Love is
a time of enchantment:
in it all days are fair and all fields
green. Youth is blest by it,
old age made benign:
the eyes of love see
roses blooming in December,
and sunshine through rain. Verily
is the time of true-love
a time of enchantment — and
Oh! how eager is woman
to be bewitched!

GIRL EXECUTIVE

Lindabelle Lantz determined to prove that her family was honorable, and she herself as good as anyone, when Rosston Miller's parents objected to their son's romance with her. Since financial security seemed to be the Miller's chief yardstick of success, Lindabelle felt she had won the first battle in the war when her father was able to buy his own farm and become a landowner. The next step was to establish herself in a career: planning menus and supplying meals to diners who had to eat alone.

Books by Jeanne Bowman
in the Ulverscroft Large Print Series:

NEIGHBORHOOD NURSE

JEANNE BOWMAN

GIRL EXECUTIVE

Complete and Unabridged

ULVERSCROFT
Leicester

First published in the
United States of America

First Large Print Edition
published December 1993

British Library CIP Data

Bowman, Jeanne
  Girl executive.—Large print ed.—
Ulverscroft large print series: romance
I. Title
813.52 [F]

ISBN 0–7089–2982–6

Published by
F. A. Thorpe (Publishing) Ltd.
Anstey, Leicestershire

Set by Words & Graphics Ltd.
Anstey, Leicestershire
Printed and bound in Great Britain by
T. J. Press (Padstow) Ltd., Padstow, Cornwall

This book is printed on acid-free paper

1

RAIN fell with steady monotony outside the Mercer Home Appliance Company windows. Lindabelle Lantz, stenographer, loved every drop of it.

Far back in her memory lurked a fear of the sun, a sun that shone without mercy day after endless day. It shriveled every blade of grass, sucked up every inch of precious moisture.

The sun, Lindabelle would have told you, was the instrument which had reduced her father from a self-respecting landowner with house and cattle and crops to an itinerant laborer who had crept halfway across the continent in the only asset he had left: a battered car loaded with bedding, pots and kettles and kids.

"This blasted weather!" exploded a voice behind her, and Lindabelle looked up at her employer, young Robert Mercer. "Didn't mean to startle you," he apologized, "but how can one expect women to buy our equipment when they can't get out of their homes without pontoons?"

Lindabelle studied the scowling young man with commiseration. Rob hadn't wanted to inherit his grandfather's retail store. He'd wanted a chance to do big things in a big way; salesmanship on a wholesale basis, with travel and the promotion of interesting sales campaigns. And here he was stuck with a downtown store until his younger brother and sister were through college and launched on careers. What was even more devastating to his morale, he'd inherited just when the recession got well under way.

"You might take the business to the customers," Lindabelle observed thoughtfully. "You might divide the suburbs into zones, send salesmen out to scout for washing hung on porches or in garages."

"Do that in words of one syllable," Mercer demanded.

"In these days of houses without basements or attics, women trying to dry laundry in the old-fashioned way

2

should be desperately eager for automatic dryers. If you could set up some deal that wouldn't wreck their budgets — "

"Say no more," murmured Mercer and, picking up a discarded tear sheet, solemnly fashioned a paper crown and placed it on his stenographer's brow at a rakish angle.

In another moment he was streaking through the store calling an impromptu sales meeting, and Lindabelle had returned to her work and her thoughts.

Here she was still a stenographer, yet she knew more about this business than anyone in the store. That was all right. Mercer senior had appreciated her ability and her knowledge, but he was of the old school. In his eyes women had become a necessary evil in business, but you didn't let them know how important they were by giving them titles. Instead you kept raising their pay so they wouldn't leave you to go to some other firm.

Lindabelle preferred pay to titles. Just as she'd shortened her inherited name Lindabelle to Linbel, so had she shortened all her personal desires. With every other member of her family, she was

3

earning all she could, and saving more than she should, toward that glorious day which now loomed directly ahead.

But that day would be only the first that would require underwriting. There would be more ahead before she could marry Rosston Miller. It was going to take money, lots of it, to stamp out his mother's objections; money, lots of it, to stamp out her memory of his mother's shocked, "Marry Linbel? A fruit tramp? An Okie? The daughter of a migrant laborer? Ross, you couldn't do that to your family."

Ross had treated this lightly. Let him get through college and find a good job. They'd marry with or without his mother's blessing. She'd come around to their way of thinking. Hadn't she treated Linbel like a daughter during the two years Linbel had worked for her?

Linbel, ever honest, had countered, "Naturally. I cooked, cleaned, washed and ironed for board, room and twenty dollars a month so I could finish high school. Don't you remember the fit she'd throw each summer when I'd move back to the migrant labor camp because I had

4

to make enough 'in the fruit' to buy clothes and books?"

The only way to win Mrs. Miller's approval was to meet her on an even economic footing.

Linbel glanced at the clock. Noon, and still raining. She glanced hungrily at an electric sign across the street. On a day like this, what she wouldn't give for a deep bowl of thick soup, preferably gumbo, piping hot. Some day she'd again have all of the food she could eat, and the kind she preferred.

Remembering how she'd gorged when she first went to the Miller farm, she was a little ashamed. But migrant labor families tried to make up for the lean months ahead by living 'high on the hog' when food was available.

Sighing deeply, she reached into her handbag for her lunch, a health sandwich. A small cellophane bag of limp raw vegetables came next. Seasoning salt made these palatable. At least her one extravagance would be hot: a small thermos containing the remains of her breakfast coffee.

At four o'clock the salesmen returned,

their eyes wide with amazement. Three had made outright sales. There were five live prospects, women who wanted to discuss the purchases with their husbands.

Mercer listened to their reports and came over to Linbel. "You," he informed her, "deserve a raise."

For one awful moment she was tempted; then she gave a decisive, "No. We can't afford it. This is only a drop in the bucket. When the rains stop, that bucket can run dry."

"But with you giving me ideas, we can move other appliances. It's right you should share in the value of your ideas."

"Later," she compromised. "We don't know what next winter will bring. Sales will go up during the seasonal upswing, but who knows what can happen to contract payments if unemployment strikes next winter?"

"That's negative thinking," he chided.

"It's common sense," she retorted, "at least until the Mercer Home Appliance Company has enough capital to carry it through another winter of recession."

She wanted to tell him she was an expert on lean winters. Even though the Lantzes had followed the harvest south to the desert, her family had known cold nights when they huddled together because there'd been no food, no reserve capital, to provide body heat.

"I believe you care more about the survival of the company than I do," commented Mercer thoughtfully.

Linbel felt miserable. She didn't care a continental about Mercer's except as it affected her own future.

"I don't," she returned painfully. "I like my job and my pay, and I'm selfish enough to want you to stay in business for these purely personal reasons."

Rob Mercer's handsome face expressed momentary chagrin; then he laughed. "Such honesty can be devastating, Linbel, but I like it. However, am I to assume you'd take another better paying position elsewhere if it were offered?"

"No," she replied, "I wouldn't be of as much value any place else. Your grandfather wouldn't admit to himself or anyone else how rapidly his health was failing, so gradually I found myself

7

taking over more and more of his work. I wouldn't be given that opportunity under any other circumstances."

He started to ask if marriage might not do, but stopped in time. Linbel was attractive, he told himself. That is, she *could* be. Brown eyes, black brows and lashes, and sand-colored hair. Not blond nor reddish, but actually desert sand-colored, the faintest tinge of brown lifting it from drabness.

She had a good complexion, actual color of her own in cheeks and lips and, he imagined, a good figure. Ah, that was it: she didn't know how to dress. As far back as he could remember, and he'd visited his grandfather many times in the three years Linbel had been with Mercer's, he'd never seen the girl in anything but a skirt and blouse.

Now take Olivia Oliver. There was a girl who knew how to make the most of every attribute. Of course Olivia leaned heavily on her father's money. He remembered accidentally overhearing a first-of-the-month row between father and daughter.

"It isn't whether or not I have the

money that matters, Livia," Mr. Oliver had stormed. "What young man will marry you if he knows he'll be subsidizing half the dress shops and furriers in the city? What do you do with all of these clothes? You couldn't wear them."

She'd insisted she did wear them a few times, then contributed to charity by giving them to such institutions as the Salvation Army and the Migrant Workers' Stores.

And Mr. Oliver, who was on a committee sponsoring the welfare of migrant workers groaned. "A hundred-dollar dress for ten cents. And what good would one of your frocks do those poor youngsters?"

Glancing at the clock, Rob had a final memory of that episode: Olivia's light assurance it gave the girls something gay and pretty they couldn't have had otherwise.

Linbel was gathering papers together, filing them away neatly. "The pay checks are here, Mr. Mercer. Mark had them made up ready for your signature before he left for the hospital."

"You mean he's ill and didn't tell me?"

"No, but if you don't smoke cigars, keep away from him in the morning. Oh, and here are your sales reports. Mr. Mercer, you've forgotten. I'm taking tomorrow off."

"You are? I mean you are, of course." And for no reason at all he began wondering why. Some stenographers took a day off to get married. But if she'd been engaged — and he didn't remember seeing a ring — why had her fiancé never been around, say at closing time?

The rain which had started by drops and gone on to buckets was now literally falling by the barrel full.

"Hadn't I better run you home?" he asked anxiously.

Linbel hesitated. Bus fare had gone up to twenty cents. Ordinarily she walked, but wet shoes were spoiled shoes, and she had no rubbers.

Mercer watched a scarlet flush mount from Linbel's throat to her brow.

"Come on," he ordered sternly.

In the car, he asked if she'd be where he could reach her by telephone and then wondered what he'd said. Why, the girl looked positively radiant.

"I'm afraid not. I'm taking the train down the valley to meet my folks; they're coming up from the south. My father," she said proudly, "is going to buy a farm."

In his relief Mercer became jocular. "And I expect he needs you there to double-check the business end."

"How did you know?" she asked, surprised.

"If I didn't I should have," he replied lamely.

He pulled up before the building she indicated, an apartment house he would have called drab. But then he knew nothing of dreams, and what beautiful colors could be used in drapes and walls and the coverings of old furniture.

Linbel said a polite thank you to her employer, then hurried in. That health sandwich hadn't stayed with her. She was downright hungry.

In her apartment, Linbel surveyed her food closet unhappily. There wasn't a thing there fit for a body to eat. That was the trouble with living alone; nothing came in small enough portions save beans and macaroni and a few minor vegetables.

Cook up a decent meal, and you were feeding it to the garbage can long before you'd eaten your way through.

"I'd like to talk to these cannery men," she thought angrily, and then shook her head. It wouldn't do any good. She of all people should know canneries were located in harvest areas, 'two hours from field to can,' to save nutrition and handling costs. Just how could a completely balanced meal go into a can small enough for one person?

Later, squeezed into the tiny dinette, she surveyed her small grill plate with distaste, then glanced out the window. The rain had stopped, and above the airshaft a single star shone in a blue-green sky.

"Star bright, star light
First star I see tonight
I wish I may, I wish I might
Have the wish I wish tonight."

Laughing at her childishness, she said quickly, "I wish to provide good food for One-Alones."

And then she frowned.

2

LINBEL awakened to find the skies cloudy again. She was glad.

"Buying a farm is like buying a hat," she told her mirrored reflection as she pulled a beret over her sandy hair. "If everything is at its best, you're never prepared for it at its worst."

Riding a train was a new experience to Linbel. In actual mileage she had traveled more than most girls of her age, but that mileage had been run up in a series of cars each better than its predecessor and, as the members of the family married off or left the migrant worker class to take steady jobs, roomier.

Rose, the eldest, had married a well-to-do realtor. Linbel felt sorry for her. Rose, who hadn't had one half Linbel's education, was so conscious of her lack she was doing everything possible to cut away all remembrance of her childhood.

She'd dropped the Lou from Rose, and she was so busy deleting colloquialisms

13

from her vocabulary she invariably used them at the wrong time. Linbel used them deliberately.

"They're so much more expressive," she explained.

"But when you use them people know you're an Okie," Rose had cried.

"I'm not, so what does it matter? Oh, I know I was born in Oklahoma, and I'm proud of it. A teacher explained an Okie to a class one day when some of us were being ribbed.

"During the first of the Dust Bowl days, some wit thought up the term Okie to cover all of the people who came to California seeking work; people who'd been defeated by the elements and had brought their families to a land of plenty.

"Because the Dust Bowl took in several states where people used their derivation of a southern accent, they were all classified under the heading of the first migrants.

"Now, thirty years later, the term is used to cover anyone who's been defeated. Our family wasn't defeated."

Rose had tried to have the last word.

"You know very well Okies have a bad reputation."

"I haven't noticed penitentiaries in other states closing out for want of customers. Maybe we feel things more deeply and make more noise about what we do, and when we rebel against circumstances we let the world know.

"Besides," she'd smiled at Rose, "who in this country has any right to crow over his birth-place? We're the most migrant nation in the world. And remember, when anyone goes state-proud on you, their ancestors had to cross the water to get here in the beginning, unless they were Indians. And if you go back into history far enough, you'll learn even they came from some other continent originally."

Rose and her well-to-do husband had been willing to add many dollars to the family farm pot.

Then there was her brother Lance. Lance Lantz being too much for high school wits, he'd changed his name to Lanny. Lanny had managed three years of high school by becoming apprenticed to a butcher. At the end of the three

15

years he'd succumbed to the lure of becoming a salesman for a wholesale packing house.

Lanny, now twenty-six, wanted to marry, but first he wanted the family settled.

There was another brother, younger than herself, who had remained with the family as a migrant worker. Calvert had spent his winters studying agriculture, his working summers studying the methods of farmers and orchardists wherever they were harvesting.

There were two younger sisters. Linbel looked out of the train window and sighed. They were out of the foothills now and speeding down through the wide valley, and no matter where she looked Linbel could remember having worked there at some time.

Now right across here, over the river and a few miles on the other side, was Eola Village. There they'd always had a real house to live in. The village was run by the government. Civic-minded people, alerted by the Council of Church Women, provided entertainment, books and a store where clothing, good clothing, could be

16

purchased for almost nothing.

Linbel sighed again. She was aware that not too far away was another type of migrant camp. And when she thought of her beautiful sister, Cassie, now called Candy, she knew they *had* to buy a farm right away. Candy was 'going Okie.'

The baby, a tow-headed five, wouldn't have to face Candy's temptations. That was good. The baby, Janice, was like herself. She took life too seriously.

More miles rolled by, and wistfully Linbel looked at the great farms, hundreds of acres hiring hundreds of pickers. Imagine her father being able to own something like one of those.

That was out of the question. In the first place, the land was priced too high for the Lantz family. In the second, the cost of equipment to cultivate and harvest was beyond even Linbel's wildest dreams. In the third, capital was needed to run such gigantic projects.

No, they couldn't afford more than a hundred and sixty to two hundred acres. They were going to pay cash, and there was to be no mortgage under any circumstances. This way the absent members of the family would be assured the others would have a roof and food from the ground."

In mid-morning the train came hooting into a small town and settled like a plate at the foot of low mountains.

The family was all there, lined up along the platform eagerly searching train windows.

Linbel counted them off. Her mother looked rested. But then she usually did in the winter. Her father stood proudly. Lanny looked a little out of family character in his city clothes until one glanced at Rose. She was overdressed as usual. Calvert — Linbel beamed proudly as she looked at her younger brother, then gave a gasp of dismay when she saw Candy. Candy didn't know it, but she was headed for the depot rest room where some of that 'goo' would be washed from her face and her hair arranged in something less like a ski slide. Janice stood soberly a little distance from the others, her black eyes enormous.

In another moment Linbel was being passed from one pair of arms to another, coming to a sharp stop at Candy's. "Gee

18

whiz, you're still wearin' that same ole suit. With the money you make — "

"Most of the money I make has been going into something that will keep you from looking a little less like a candidate for the Miss Skid Row title. Come on."

"I cain't do a thing with th' girl," Mrs. Lantz complained softly. "Livin' like we do, it's nigh impossible to keep her from formin' associations with the wrong kind, her being so pretty and all."

"She certainly doesn't look pretty today." Linbel's eyes were snapping. "I'd be ashamed to introduce her to my friends."

"Ah'm high-strung like 'n 'Rabian hoss," Candy informed her loftily. "Leastwise that's what I'm told."

"You're going to be hamstrung before I'm through with you," Linbel informed her. "Least-wise you'll do what someone who loves you tells you."

"I tried to tell her," Rose began stiffly, "but she paid me no mind."

Candy, her hair and face restored to some semblance of natural beauty, accompanied the rest of the family to a small café in sullen defiance.

19

Mr. Lantz looked at the pretty girl, then at Linbel, upon whom he admitted he leaned, and sighed deeply. Linbel had been a right pretty girl, too, but her black eyes were getting too snappy, and pinch-penny lines were starting to grow around her mouth.

"How's your young man?" he asked abruptly.

"Which one?" murmured Linbel absently as she scanned the menu.

"You mean you got yourself two?" cried Candy in admiration.

"Oh! Oh, no. I work for a young man now, but he's spoken for. Rosston's at college. He writes right often, but I have a time answering."

"Do we buy us this farm," murmured Mrs. Lantz, "you can marry up proper."

Linbel lay the menu card aside and looked out on the lazy little town. Marry up proper. My, what music that would have been five years ago. And of course it still was. My goodness, wasn't that one of the main reasons she wanted the family to be settled?

They asked what Rosston Miller was aiming to be, and when Linbel said he was taking business administration but might settle for an accountancy, Calvert shook his head.

"Imagine, with a farm like his'n, handed down for near a hundred years, wanting business."

Linbel looked at him anxiously. "Calvert, farming *is* business these days. You don't just prepare, plant and harvest your soil; you have to use business brains on the whole procedure. Don't ever forget that or you'll come a cropper."

They talked then of the family's winter in the citrus belt, and Mrs. Lentz said she couldn't nowise imagine spending a winter around her own stove again, with a canning closet and root bin to draw on.

Candy said if the farm was too far from town she wasn't about to stay there. She'd get her a job, and Mr. Lantz said did she try he'd tan her hide until she couldn't sit down on the job for a year.

"Not a one in this family but what's scrimped and put by to live decent, except you. You're not a-going to spoil it for the rest of us by any loose living."

"You didn't throw a fit when Lindabelle got herself a job," Candy retorted sullenly.

"Candy," Linbel leaned toward her earnestly, "I never scrimped on lunch or clothes or carfare but what I thought of you finishing high school like other girls. Believe me, hon, those extra years in school give a girl double the salary she'd earn with pick-up jobs."

"I can just see myself graduating," stormed Candy, "with all the other girls upping their noses at me and nice boys feared to take me out because — "

"But, hon, you won't be a fruit tramp any more. You'll have a permanent address."

"A permanent address." The phrase was echoed around the table, the wonder of it, the vast meaning of it in their lives touching each voice with awe.

"Let's eat up," said Mr. Lantz, his voice strong and full of pride, "a real Thanksgiving meal. Order big, all of you."

They ordered big, but what with one eye on the hands of the clock moving toward the meeting hour the real estate agent had set, none but Rose and Lanny ate much.

The great hour arrived, and the family divided into two cars, Mr. Lantz, Linbel and Calvert riding with the agent, the others getting into Lanny's car.

The agent, who'd sized up Mr. Lantz as someone whom he could push hard to move property, caught the searching glance of Linbel's black eyes and did a little reconstruction of his sales approach.

The family, Mr. Lantz had told him, had fifteen thousand dollars cash for a farm. Very well, if they had that much, he'd talk them into using it as earnest money, for if they could raise fifteen thousand cash they could raise fifty.

He used this approach on one farm; then the little sandy-haired girl turned on him.

"Mr. Brownley, my father told you exactly what he wanted. He's in full possession of his faculties. Will you show us something in that price bracket, or shall we drive back to town and contact another agent?"

"But, Miss Lantz," he defended himself, "a farm within that price range is not self-supporting. If you knew anything about farming — "

"Mr. Brownley, the farmers who are suffering these days are the ones who have expanded too much. If my father has a farm that will grow his food and pay his taxes — "

" — and no mortgage payments," put in Mr. Lantz.

"A diversified farm, like Pa said this morning," contributed Calvert.

They nearly went off the highway, because Mr. Brownley lifted both hands from the wheel in resignation.

He had only two farms such as they specified.

He took them to the first, and Linbel could just see herself getting married in the garden. It had roses falling all over an archway and blue-spiked flowers sticking up like cathedral spires . . . at least it had in her dreams. At this time of the year it had nothing but lawn and archways and a summerhouse she assumed would be covered with grapes.

"Gosh, Sis," breathed Candy, looking at the white pillars of the shaded terrace, "I could really live here."

While Mr. Lantz, the owner and the two boys went out on the farm proper, the women joined the owner's wife in the living room, where a fireplace revealed a log, paper and chips and a body could just see the firelight dancing on the brass knobs of the andirons.

The furniture 'went with.' Linbel sank onto a deep divan and came to an abrupt stop. The divan was a snare and a delusion. It was made of plywood covered with thin cushions and had not a spring to its name.

One thing for sure, she and Rosston would never sit on this couch discussing wedding plans.

"Please, Mrs. Jackart, I'd like to see how the fireplace chimney draws," Linbel said, and Mrs. Jackart quickly decided they should see the other rooms first.

Candy went from rapture to rapture at cleverly contrived conveniences, at painted walls and blossoming chintz drapes which turned out to be fibre.

And behind her came Linbel, moving a pan in the kitchen sink to find it stained copper yellow; moving a screen to find the door swung back at an angle, showing the house had listed so the door couldn't be used; touching walls and finding them wood covered with cloth and paper.

"Think I'll join the men folk," said Linbel, and went sailing out to draw her father and brothers aside.

"They've got this place dressed up for a killing," she announced. "Everything inside is sham. If they're that kind of people, then look out for the land. Two to a penny there's no water, and maybe there's a road due through. I'd not trust them to their own front gate."

Mr. Lantz nodded. "Barn looks it." And he walked back, "Mr. Brownley, we'd like to see that other place."

Mr. Brownley took an active dislike to the girl in the shabby suit. These days an agent didn't often see as much cash money as these people had, and his percentage on a fifty thousand dollar farm would have done much to ease his financial strain in this time of slow-moving real estate.

When he tried to defend the property he'd just shown, the girl told him they didn't respond to any sweet talk. "Mr. Brownley," she said seriously, "there are folk who think anyone with a southwestern accent left his brains behind when he came west.

"Every member of our family, from the baby right on up, has done without to save for the security of a paid-for roof and ground to feed us. You know what a seasonal worker's pay is, so you can figure what it's meant to save fifteen thousand in ten years. But we've figured it was worth it to become self-respecting land owners."

Brownley stopped the car and smiled at them. "I apologize," he said, and meant it. "Now I do have a place you might like. The house is sturdy but needs paint and a new porch. The outbuildings are good — "

"And the land?" asked Calvert anxiously.

"There's a big family orchard behind the house on a knoll; then the land drops to a stream. It's about that I want to speak. It floods every season, brings down silt and minerals from the glacial mountains around it. It produces the best vegetables I've ever tasted."

"How much?" demanded Mr. Lantz.

Brownley hesitated a moment, then

sighed. "It's only twelve thousand because it's so far off the beaten path. Oh, there's a school bus, but it only takes the children to country schools, a union high school of farm children. And there's a grange. But, Mr. Lantz, I'll be honest about it. I doubt if you could make a living off the place."

"Maybe western farmers can't," stated Mr. Lantz, "but I made a livin' for my brood right up to the time the dust choked up our last water hole. We'd like right smart to see this farm, Mr. Brownley."

They drove on, found a main highway and went streaking east. Farms became smaller and less prosperous-looking with each mile, yet, Linbel thought, more like homes. Farmhouses were indubitably farmhouses, with not a Spanish, New England or modernistic line on one of them.

"Scalin' down to our size," observed her father contentedly.

"I'll pull off as soon as we top this rise," Mr. Brownley said. "You can get a pretty good bird's eye view of it. Of course it's run-down now. It was part of an estate, and while none of the heirs would live there, every living one of them fought for the ownership."

"But the title's clear now?" asked Linbel.

"Definitely. And the irony of it is that most of the money derived from the sale will have to be used by the quarreling heirs to pay court costs. Well, here we are."

She wouldn't look. Linbel felt her way out of the car with the others, but she couldn't bear to open her eyes and look down and find some monstrosity.

"Well, now," breathed her father. And she thought there was that in his released breath which indicated a rocker on a veranda after a hard day's work, a pipe and a moon coming over the mountain and frogs croaking down in a pond.

Warily she opened her eyes.

3

SHE'D seen replicas of this house a hundred times since she'd been in the northwest, but not in this exact setting. It was two-storied, with roofed verandas running half along one side and half along another, giving shade or sunshine according to the need of the season.

"Clothes-dryin' space," came in a sibilant sigh from Mrs. Lantz.

"That will landscape well," observed Rose thoughtfully.

"It is," came Linbel's enigmatic reply.

Nature had already created a background, sharp upthrust hills in a half-circle to north and east, softer wooded foothills to south and west. The house was on a knoll with an orchard rising on a second knoll immediately behind; the land before it slanted to a wide shallow valley now brimming with water.

"If it can look that good on a day like this," commented Lanny, "it'll be a picture in the summer."

"I think it's *awful*," wailed Candy. "Look at it — miles from nowhere, and all drab and greyish."

Linbel slipped an arm around her sister and led her away. Candy had grown up while things were easier for the Lantzes, the older children were able to support themselves, leaving a little more for the younger ones. And if that real estate agent hadn't shown them that deceptive house with the pillars and make-believe trimmings, the comparison wouldn't have brought so much disappointment.

"It can be painted later, Candy," she whispered, "and some lawn chairs put out front. What's more, it won't be about to fall down around your ears come a storm."

"You can talk, livin' in a swell apartment with steam heat and things."

"Candy, when I was your age I'd have given my eyeteeth for a shanty. Mostly we had tents then. You get in and work like I have, and you can have an apartment. You won't get even a shanty if you start running around with cheap folk."

31

"I'm goin' to work, and right away. I won't live out here in the sticks."

"You won't leave until you're of age," Mr. Lantz said firmly as he came up to them.

"Lindabelle did."

"Lindabelle was different," her father remarked thoughtfully. "She never lived for herself alone." He frowned, seeking words to convey his meaning. "She's always had a way of seeing things as a whole, like a — well, a six-span team with her at the reins gettin' each hoss to step in time."

"And Candy's special," Linbel said quickly, "like a flower, a beautiful one you don't want to bloom too fast because then it fades even faster."

"What's the use of blooming if nobody's ever going t' see you?" was the sullen acceptance of the compliment.

"I swear to goodness I could up-end that girl and tan her hide," muttered Mr. Lantz as they walked back to the agent's car.

"She'll root down," Linbel comforted him, "once she gets in with the other farm children."

But she'd been with farm children and hadn't been accepted as one of them. Of course her father hadn't owned a farm then. And she'd been hired help.

"Before she meets up with any of them," she sighed, throwing away her own dreams, "I'll take her to town and buy some clothes that won't peel folks' eyeballs."

Calvert aroused from his dream of a farm and smiled shyly. "Wouldn't seem lucky if we all agreed on a place. Glad it's Candy kickin'. That girl cottons to a phoney like a cocklebur to a sheep's tail."

The house didn't improve in appearance as they drove up. But Mr. Lantz called happily from the agent's car to his son's, "Mother, see those foundations? Steady as all get-out."

"I see that summer kitchen," she called back, indicating the screened porch on the north side. "I can do a mite of canning there without swelterin'."

And Linbel thought of Mercer's electric and gas ranges and discarded them for the time being. After cooking over campfires and portable gasoline stoves, a stationary wood range would provide the luxury of the familiar.

This house too was furnished. Footsteps echoing on the verandas, they walked around to the front, peering in windows, while the agent tried various keys on the door.

"A patent rocker," crooned Mrs. Lantz.

"Grandpa had one like that big wooden one, 'side the heater," Mr. Lantz contributed.

Going through the various rooms, Linbel wondered why the place seemed so much like home. She'd been not much older than Janice when they'd left Oklahoma. But listening to her mother, she realized this house had been furnished in the same era as the grandfather's home her father had inherited.

Calvert had no time for houses and only a little time for the outbuildings. He came tearing up from the lower fields, a handful of dirt outheld. "Man, this here is *soil*," he caroled.

He did take time to check on the farm equipment, and while it wasn't up-to-the minute like the type he used on other

34

men's land, it satisfied him. He could, he said, monkey with it and bring it to fare.

The agent left them on the front veranda for a family conference and walked off, a pleased smile illuminating his countenance. Maybe he could have won a higher percentage of that cash for his firm, but they'd still have had this old farm on their hands. Most people looked more for show than shoring, like that pretty younger daughter.

Now the older one, Lindabelle, was a sharp one, with plenty of sound common sense.

The Lantz family returned to the farm the next day. Mr. Brownley had called the estate administrator, and he'd said, as it was a cash purchase, by all means to give them possession.

It was pouring rain, but Mr. Lantz made quite a ritual of turning the key in the front door for the first time. And they didn't need sun, Linbel thought; the radiance on her parent's faces lighted the whole gloomy valley.

After an early dinner her father took her aside for a private talk.

"Well, girl, we're off your shoulders."

"Pa, this has been a whole family project."

"Oh, yes, but do you think ary a one of us would have stuck it out if you hadn't been at the reins? Now you get busy and marry up with that young man o' yourn before your romance runs dry."

"He won't finish college before June; then he has to find a job. His folks won't help him because he wouldn't take over the farm." She couldn't tell her father it was because he insisted upon marrying the daughter of a fruit tramp. "They're planning to turn everything over to his younger brother, who likes farming."

"Well, don't fiddle-faddle around. He's a good-looking lad. Some other girl's apt to step in and talk him into liking a farm."

She'd carried the threat of that like a thorn in her heart. Hearing it put into words pressed it deeper. Maybe she should have arranged to stop off at the university town en route back to the city. But she couldn't bring herself to let Rosston see her in the same old suit, not

36

on the campus where girls made a career of looking pretty.

When she left, her father poked some folded bills into her hands. "Here. Now that we've got this place cheaper, seems we can afford to buy you some glad rags. Spend this on yourself, Lindabelle, or I'll be downright put out with you."

Linbel estimated the sum he'd given her and saw it as a long succession of walks to and from work; of buying second day rolls, margarine instead of butter, and hamburger.

She felt she should turn it back, then tipped her chin with pride. Her father, a landowner, had been able to give her fifty dollars. It gave dignity to them both.

Lanny drove Rose and Linbel into town to catch their trains. Each would travel in an opposite direction. He confided he had been worried about a market for such diversified farm products.

"But Brownley tells me there's a fair-sized freezer plant in town here that will take everything. He says fruits and vegetables don't grow to the size they do in the big valley, but they've better quality, more flavor. And lots of people want them because the minerals here are supposed to give more nutrition."

Each then talked of what they would do now that the family was settled. Rose wanted to take a course in landscaping so she could shine in the City Garden Club. And Lanny would, of course, marry. It was, he said, a downright miracle the way his Judy had waited for him.

"When are you and Rosston going to hitch up?" he asked Linbel.

She wasn't sure, but now that she had a home address and a place to be married in, she could make definite plans. "Next fall, I guess."

Rose had never met Rosston, and Linbel brought out her billfold and showed her the photograph of a tall, slender young man with curling blond hair and laughing eyes. Rose looked from the photograph to Linbel, and one could sense she wondered what he had seen in this drab little sister of hers.

"You can bring him down for a weekend when you get a vacation," she offered generously.

Going home, a dark landscape offering

nothing to distract her attention, Linbel leaned back in the chair and dreamed. The Millers would come to the wedding, and they'd see her people were of substance and property. Maybe the place would seem a little shabby to them, but it would be sound. There'd be no flimflam, no covering up.

Her father would treat them with dignity, and surely anyone with half an eye could tell her mother came of good Virginia stock.

Rosston had said, "Linbel, forget families. It's us, that's all."

But she knew better.

And Ross had said, "The trouble with you is that you think too much. You have to see everything as a whole."

Maybe, but she'd been right thus far. She'd refused to elope with him the night after high school graduation. Now they were both better prepared to meet life, he with an education, she with valuable business experience.

Maybe a Christmas wedding, she thought, putting the date off another three months from the autumn date she'd halfway planned. There'd be snow, and the house wouldn't show how much it needed painting.

It wasn't raining when she reached the city and, without thinking it was no longer necessary, Linbel walked to her apartment.

She was nearly there before she realized this was no way for the daughter of a man of property to act. She was going to have to break herself of this pinch-penny habit.

She did the next morning. For the first time since she had gone to work for the Mercer Home Appliance Company, Linbel took a bus downtown. But what was more important, her deep handbag carried neither a sandwich nor a thermos bottle.

She, Linbel Lantz, was going to walk across the street at noon and slide onto a stool and then order a hot lunch.

All of the way downtown she thought of her job ahead, its importance to her. She could now save one hundred a month and have enough left over to buy a few clothes. She could watch sales and begin picking up a few good pieces of linen, blankets, pillows. Girls still brought filled linen chests to their marriage, didn't they? That is, if they didn't elope when they were too young.

Mrs. Miller had. She'd told Linbel all she'd brought to her husband's home, a dozen of everything. Of course she still had some of those dozens left, unused and yellowing with age.

On the bus were other stenographers, and Linbel could almost tell by looking at them how much they made each week.

And her own pay check assumed greater importance. On their salary she wouldn't be able to save, and there'd be no hope chest, no dowry.

"I'll just have to bear down on young Rob," she thought, reaching the store and finding she was the first one there except for the boys in the delivery department. "And I'll have to plan ways and means of moving this stock. I'll sign up for a night course in advertising and public relations."

In another moment she was swamped by demands of men anxious to be about their duties and with no one in the front but herself to direct them.

"Do we dare dock the salesmen's

41

wages?" she asked the bookkeeper who slid in at the last moment, yawning over the weariness of having become a father two days before. There had been, Linbel noticed, celebrations unattended by mother and son.

Now he faced her seriously. "No, that wouldn't work. But I'm telling you this, Linbel: if the boys don't settle down there'll be no wages to dock. We'll inch through summer all right, but if there's no business pick-up we can't ride the winter."

The salesmen appeared and lolled about.

Morning passed with no sign or word of Robert Mercer. One of the salesmen said young Rob had spoken of some big deal pending and they'd all taken heart from that.

Linbel heard it with a premonitory shudder and began to wish she'd made a sandwich. And she clutched the thought of that fifty dollars and almost didn't take part of her lunch hour to window-shop.

It was four o'clock when Mercer came in, carrying triumph like a visible aura about him.

"Gather around, lads," he cried, assembling his sales force. "I've big news. I've just bought a carload of home freezers, little ones we can't help selling."

Linbel's head dropped on her elbow-propped hand. Little ones. Hadn't she been through that with his grandfather? People who could afford deep freezes invested in big ones only.

Well, goodbye, Mercer Home Appliance Company. Goodbye, savings account. And if her family needed money, goodbye, marriage.

4

ONLY one of the older salesmen realized what young Mercer had done and, because he'd been with Rob's grandfather for years, told him.

"I hope you haven't closed that deal," he said hurriedly.

And then he tried to explain. They'd learned, here at Mercer's, that in this locality, housewives who wanted to keep only a minimum of frozen foods on hand purchased the combination refrigerator-freezer. It was, he elucidated, a matter of floor space.

These very combination units they had on the floor would hold nearly as much frozen food as the cabinet freezers Mercer had just purchased.

"But we'll educate them in the economy of bulk buying," cried Mercer, only slightly deflated. "For instance, when beef is down they can buy a half a beef, have it cut and frozen for storage."

"Son," sighed Thurman, the old salesman, "a family buying that size freezer wouldn't have the need of even a fore-quarter, unless they intended to live on nothing else. That's what I'm trying to get over to you."

Mercer turned to Linbel, his dark blue eyes pleading for the help she'd always given in an emergency.

"He means," she said after a moment, "there'd be no variety. The freezer is too small for a small family to indulge in bulk buying for it."

And she wondered what kind of a sales talk had been offered to make Mercer invest so much capital, needed elsewhere, in such a venture.

He told her after the others had dispersed. "The freezers were brought out for a new apartment house; then the contractor went broke and the outfit taking over the job refused the order. I got them at a terrific reduction because they were eating up profits in the warehouse.

"It's too late for me to back out," he continued thoughtfully. "I signed up Saturday afternoon and deposited the check to go with the contract this

45

morning. Short of finding the goods faulty, I have no out."

"We'll work out something," she murmured, but her heart wasn't in it.

The bookkeeper offered to drive her home, the hospital containing his wife and new son being in that direction, and Linbel accepted gratefully.

When they drew up in front, Linbel sat on, and they discussed their problem. Mercer's, on paper, was most solvent, but unhappily the Mercer Home Appliance Company's solvency was based upon contracts calling for monthly payments. People whose credit rating was A-1 could be helpless to keep that status if they were out of work for any length of time.

"All that repossessed appliances mean to us these days is something taking up needed floor space," he commented gloomily. "And with cut-rate houses selling new goods at what we'd have to ask on a resale — " And then he broke off with, "What possessed young Rob?"

"He isn't married," murmured Linbel. After a moment she explained, "He's always had everything he wanted. He

46

hasn't lived at home enough really to know the cost of running a home. To him sales resistance isn't fear of not being able to meet payments; it's something to overcome, a choice of his goods over his competitors.'"

Slowly then she left the car, looking back with a thoughtful, "I'll think up something."

Still preoccupied, she took a letter from her box and went up, changed to the comfort of a housecoat, then decided to put dinner on the stove before she allowed herself the luxury of reading the bi-weekly message from Rosston.

"Oh," she said angrily when she looked into the small refrigerator and then into her food closet, "there isn't anything there. Why didn't I remember I hadn't shopped Saturday?"

And then she thought, Now if I just had one of those little freezers —

There was a thought. If she had one she could take some Saturday afternoon or Sunday and prepare a succession of meals; then when she came home from work all she would have to do was pop one in the oven. Of course she could go out and buy the ready-made frozen dinners to stock such a freezer, but the cost was something to think about.

"Besides," she muttered, "there are never enough vegetables."

And then she looked around the apartment and wondered where she could put such an appliance. Of course hers was the smallest in the building, an after-thought of the contractor to give that much more rental space.

Opening cans, she wondered how many hundreds of girls and young men, and perhaps widows and widowers, were preparing the same sort of more or less tasteless meals. And ofttimes money wasn't the concern.

Roasts and stews and meat loaves, she thought. By the time one-alone eats his way through they've lost their savor. Or else they've been thrown in the garbage can. As for pies and cakes —

Well, it wouldn't be too long now before her hamburger days would be over. Another nine or ten months, and as Mrs. Rosston Miller she'd be preparing all of the tasty meals she'd learned how to prepare in his mother's kitchen.

Pots bubbling gently on the little range, Linbel sat down at the narrow table and opened Rosston's letter, and a small cry of delight rang out.

"Oh, he's got a job already."

At a plywood mill the moment he graduated, he wrote. It wasn't what he wanted, but his class had been advised to take what they could get this year and write it off to experience.

"The way you handle money, we can make it," he wrote, "and if we're together we won't care whether or not we have all of the latest gadgets."

Later, down in the laundry room, Linbel listened to the chatter of the young working wives who lived in the larger apartments.

"And he told Ben buying appliances now before we bought a house was like money in the bank. We'd be buying with the market down. But I told Ben that by the time we got us a house maybe they'd be giving away washing machines as a gimmick to get you to buy bed linens."

"Like they give a whole freezerful of food to get you to buy a freezer?" asked another.

"I knew a couple who bought that deal." A third turned from the dryer. "They ate up the food, then moved off, leaving the freezer behind. Two hundred dollars worth of food, and they'd only made a couple of payments. The food people had had a deal with the freezer outfit, but it didn't do them no good. The freezer people repossessed the freezer, but there wasn't a darn thing the frozen food people could do about repossessing what wasn't there any more."

Linbel's hopes, which had gone up momentarily, dropped again. And then she thought of what these young working wives faced each night, a rush home to prepare dinner. Now if they had one of the new freezers Mercer had just bought —

"You work for an appliance outfit, don't you, Linbel?" one asked.

Linbel nodded thoughtfully. "And we have a wonderful buy on apartment-house-sized freezers. Now, just for the book, I'm not trying to sell you. But for research, would you invest in one?"

Each said she wouldn't and each gave a different reason, though the basic one was the same. One, who worked for a furniture store, expressed it more fully.

"Apartment house dwellers are different here from what they are in lots of cities," she explained. "The furniture men's association made a survey and found that only one percent had any intention of remaining, and this one percent lived in apartment-hotels.

"All of the rest were waiting until they could buy in the suburbs or in the country. That was the reason, they found, that furnished apartments were more popular than the unfurnished ones. Couples said they didn't know what they would want until they found the house it would go into. Besides, with mover's fees as they are, why pay for moving heavy stuff if they wanted to try out different apartments before they settled?"

And that, thought Linbel, took care of the sale of the freezers to apartment house dwellers, for there they would have the heaviest of all appliances to move.

Linbel, her laundry completed, returned to write a quick note to Rosston, first to congratulate him on his first offer of a position, then to tell of the purchase of the farm, her father's purchase of a farm.

Rereading his letter, she noticed one line she had overlooked. Rosston was planning a trip up during mid-term.

At first she was filled with familiar consternation at her shabby appearance. At school, where she'd taken the Bishop sewing course, she'd managed to look the equal of her classmates. But here — what would he think?

She thought of her father's gift, but fifty dollars wouldn't go far. And then she remembered the farm, a *fait accompli*.

She wouldn't start saving for another month. Her salary, plus the gift, would allow for a street dress, coat and hat and hair styling. Long ago she had let it grow to save the cost of cutting and waving.

But when she lay in her narrow bed her thoughts were on neither the clothes, the farm nor Rosston. She concentrated upon what to do about the Mercer Home Appliance Company.

Morning brought little help; a cold rain was still falling. It splashed on the window sill beside her breakfast table and jeered at the idea of a mere stenographer being able to do what presumably sound business men couldn't.

Yet young Rob's grandfather had not only listened to her; he'd gradually let her present ideas and then put them into effect — under his name, of course.

That gave her one idea. If I could work out some over-all plan, then tell young Rob and the others that it was old Mr. Mercer's, they'd accept it. And it wouldn't be lying, really, because it was old Mr. Mercer who taught me to see the business as a whole.

Young Mr. Mercer came in blithely, his confidence restored. He'd spent the evening with Olivia Oliver and his mother, and they'd come up with a promotion plan he would put into effect immediately.

Linbel shuddered even before she heard the plan. She had been told Olivia Oliver had taken Home Economy at college, but she doubted if she were economical in her outlook.

"We'll start immediately; have to get some of our money back," began Rob Mercer. "We'll buy up television time and really go to town on 'A Freezer in

Every Apartment.'"

Some of the salesmen were listening, and Linbel had to swallow painfully before she could speak. She didn't want to dash their hopes.

"You mean you'll take the television time after your men have made a quick run-down on how many apartments have room enough for the freezer," she commented as though it were a foregone fact. "Of course people could put them in their dinettes and move their dinette sets to the living rooms."

"Not in my apartment," stated one salesman. "And having seen the type we've bought, a long narrow chest, I doubt if it would be done in many others."

Another said they might make it in his if his wife would give up her cedar chest in the bedroom. "But you'd have to convince her it was worth the sacrifice, with a market on the corner two hops and a skip from the foyer."

"The sad part," bemoaned another who'd seen a photograph of the new appliance, "is that this contractor had a chain of apartments going up. His architect designed a kitchen to fit the freezers, then had the freezers especially made. They're not only stuck with them here, but in several other west coast cities."

"How about the holding company that took over the apartments?" Linbel asked hopefully, "Couldn't we sell to them?"

"Nope. They said it was a crackpot idea and one of the reasons the contractor folded. They could refuse the freezers because they were not an integral part of the building proper, and they've already turned the chest space into cabinets."

Linbel beamed at the youngest salesman, who'd taken time and effort to look into the background of the purchase.

"What was Miss Oliver's promotion plan?" Linbel asked.

"'Make your Sunday drives pay for your groceries,'" murmured Mercer.

Something struck the window panes, and all heads turned. The rain had turned to sleet.

The oldest salesman spoke soothingly. "There's time to consider. In this country, roadside stands in the country don't open up until June or really get under way until early July. This is February, with possible snow forecast. Right now apartment dwellers are ranting at the janitor for more heat. They're not thinking of driving in the country. Now take early May — "

"But this is a wonderful time to sell dryers," Linbel spoke up. The men glared at her and then, laughing, went for rainproof coats. All but the oldest, who would handle the chance customers, darted out in the storm.

When the place quieted, Mercer returned to stare down at Linbel. "Those men believe anything you tell them," he charged.

Anxiously she looked up, wished something could be done about one lock of hair that wouldn't respond even to a crew cut; knew there wasn't and sighed.

"Not me," she corrected, "but your grandfather's stenographer. You see your grandfather rode out a lot of ups and downs in the business market. He was barely started when the 1907 depression struck. Then his business was so light he could ride easily.

"His hard time came in the early thirties. He had invested heavily in refrigerators, which were quite new then. But he came through."

"How?" asked Mercer abruptly. "Oh, I know, I heard him tell about it. That was when Dad was alive and I thought he'd be taking over the business, not me."

Carefully Linbel chose her words. "He knew to a penny how much money he had to count on to carry him over a given period. He watched business trends, knew what his competitors were doing and estimated his seasonal income and outgo."

"Where do you come into this?"

Linbel shrugged and smiled. "I think I've heard him talk so much I even use his voice, and the men remember it and forget it isn't he talking."

He left moodily, and swiftly Linbel wrote a note and slipped it to the bookkeeper. "Suggest reply to requested report be on annual basis. Break into seasons and show decrease in last two years upon which to base the balance of this year."

Perhaps she was overstepping, but if

she had interested young Rob into asking for a financial run-down of any kind, the bookkeeper would be ready with what he needed to know.

And somehow Linbel felt he should have this before his next meeting with Olivia Oliver.

At noon Linbel marched defiantly to the café across the street. She was going to have the rest of this month to herself. She could save afterwards. And she deliberately and with malice aforethought ordered the dollar and a half special.

For some reason she felt much better, but when she returned to her office and found how little work she had to do, her spirits plummeted.

True, Mercer had asked for a report. The bookkeeper showed Linbel a copy of what he'd given him. And her spirits went even lower.

"Of course," soothed the bookkeeper, "this is the lowest quarter of the year for appliance sales."

"And the lowest year of the lowest quarter of the lowest sales," muttered Linbel. "How did Mr. Mercer react?"

"He was deflated. He asked for more details, and then he wanted to know why businessmen were talking promotion to overcome recession. I told him that was an excellent idea when there was enough capital to push the bicycle up the hill."

Linbel blinked at him, then grasped the idea.

"I told him his grandfather had made a success of the business by knowing when to brake and when to pedal."

"Beautiful," beamed Linbel, and planned to make up a small poster and send it to the farm. "What did he say?"

"Well," confided the young man, "he said he guessed buying those freezers was pedaling downhill. If he could find a brake he'd use it before we all landed on our noses."

At her desk, Linbel sat staring at her notebook, then ran a nervous hand over her hair.

"Miss Lantz!" Linbel jumped and wheeled her chair around to find Rob Mercer and the beautiful Miss Oliver standing there. "Miss Lantz, can you convince Miss Oliver that this is not the time to put on a food clinic and a television show to promote those fool freezers I bought?"

Linbel looked at Olivia Oliver's face and wondered if anyone could stop her.

5

"**I**T isn't as though Dad wouldn't back you," Olivia was saying.

Linbel shuddered again. Let the Oliver money come into Mercer's, and it would cease being Mercer's, to say nothing of one Linbel Lantz ceasing to be affiliated with the former Mercer's in any capacity.

"Linbel — " prompted Mercer, his pleading tone now acute.

"I think it's a wonderful idea," said Linbel guilelessly. "The freezing season doesn't start until the middle of June in this area. That would give Miss Oliver five months to screen writers; have them make up their scripts; choose a producer; get her cast together; and of course buy the right television time."

For the first time Miss Oliver looked upon her almost-fiancé's stenographer with approval. She beamed. She also looked decidedly bemused. And Linbel knew she'd had no idea so much was involved in 'putting a sales promotion problem on television.'

"But the cost — " moaned Mercer.

Linbel nodded. "By that time Mercer's should be in a position to absorb it. Miss Oliver, being the only girl in this firm, I've been trying to apply feminine psychology to sales promotion. I wonder if you'd mind checking some of the ideas I thought I might suggest to Mr. Mercer."

"I'd love it," cried Olivia Oliver. "I gave my all to Home Economy at college. Actually, I hadn't a flair for any of the finer arts — "

"Are there any finer?" Linbel asked innocently.

"I really wouldn't know." Olivia accepted the chair Rob brought up. "My father has always been in the food business, first as a chain store owner, then as a wholesaler. I've heard food from the time I was old enough to know what it meant. Now, what are these ideas?"

Linbel discussed seasonal sales in home appliances, and when she was through Olivia was convinced she herself had thought of the ideas. That was what

Linbel wanted: something to divert her from that costly television program.

Rob showed interest, but the one concentrating the most heavily was the bookkeeper, who seemed absorbed in other business.

"When you can't whip 'em, win 'em over?" he asked dryly as the others left. He added admiringly, "Women."

But Mercer hadn't seen through the ruse. Mercer hadn't been married and had spent little time at home during his reasoning years.

"At least," was his comment next morning, "I didn't have that TV program dinned into my ears all evening." And then he looked at Linbel, who was studying her hands with absorbed interest. "Why, you little minx."

"I thought," Linbel defended herself quickly, "that once she understood your business better, she wouldn't be so quick to jeopardize it."

She wanted to tell him that the sooner he married her the better off he'd be. Then she wondered if he would.

"The trouble with trouble," Linbel informed a small hamburger loaf she

63

was wrapping in aluminum foil, "is that it is so involved."

As she prepared dinner she reviewed the day, thinking of the clothes she planned to buy on Saturday; the appointment with the hair stylist; and the low ebb of her bank account.

The hamburger roll came out of the pan and its wrapping, a savory bit. Of course it had taken time to prepare it; carrots had been grated, celery and onion chopped. She'd had bread crumbs handy. Seasoning salt was added with a twist of the wrist. But if all of this could have been done in advance —

Maybe she *should* purchase one of those little freezers, prepare a variety of meals in advance.

She thought of the freezers Mercer had bought as she ate her dinner, then shook her head. They weren't large enough for the economical purchase of food.

Later, when her mother had had her fill of canning, she'd buy the folks a ranch size freezer. And of course when she and Rosston set up housekeeping, if and when they were able to buy a home, they'd have one.

Which reminded her she must begin planning a dinner for Rosston when he arrived over the weekend. Not that he wouldn't want to dine out, but she'd never before been able to invite him into a home of her own.

'And an attractive house dress,' she added to her list of purchases, 'pink.'

For a little while she sat dreaming of 'Ross' and his gay spirit, which seemed so at variance with the popular conception of an accountant, business manager, bookkeeper.

She thought of all she would have to tell him: about the farm, principally. Washing dishes, she found herself talking to him. "An ideal spot, Ross, with a little freezer plant in a nearby town which will take all of the fruit and vegetables they can raise."

She wouldn't tell him she was free to marry, now that the 'folks were off her shoulders,' because she never thought of it that way.

Rosston thought her beautiful that Saturday. After the first swift embrace, he held her off and stared. "What have you done to yourself, Linbel?" he demanded.

"You don't like me this way?" she asked anxiously.

"Like you?" he cried. "Darling girl, I loved you the way you were. Now I don't know that it's going to be safe to leave you around for other men to look at. Your hair — what happened?"

Linbel was radiant. "Had it styled, cut and waved, that sort of thing. Now any hat will look good."

"That one does."

It did. A compromise between winter and spring, it slanted over one heavy wave in a debonair fashion that really did something for her spirit.

It was copper-colored, with a sand-colored bow; and her suit was copper brown, her accessories sand color, so that even her sandy hair took on copper highlights.

Some of Rosston's classmates clustered around, and proudly he introduced her, saying, "Sorry, fellows; she's been bespoke for lo these many years."

They dined out that night, and Linbel thought happily that while she'd never doubted Rosston's love, he would not formerly have introduced her to his

66

classmates with that possessive air. On second thought, they wouldn't have cared for an introduction.

Their talk was a mélange of past, present and future. It was remember when, and now that the folks have bought a farm, and let's set a wedding date.

"No," Linbel said decisively to the last. "You don't graduate until June; then you'll be starting the new job. And until you're really settled in that it wouldn't be fair to you to have half your mind on a wife."

"Not you, Linbel. Why, honey girl, you forget we practically grew up in the same house. Having you around is like having the rest of myself handy. Together we make one. The rest of the time I go around only half myself."

"I'd like to see you put that down in figures," she chided, but her cheeks were pink and her black eyes shining.

"I could," he insisted. "We're an unbalanced account unless we're together."

"Fifty percent still owing," she conceded thoughtfully. Then she brought up another argument.

"Ross, I wanted to be married from

my home," how proudly she said that, "and I want it fixed up properly before then. Oh, not glamorized; just made to look like the home of a self-respecting farmer, which is what Dad was before the drouth."

"Well, I have a little —"

"No! Thank you, but no. I don't want you ever to feel you're taking on my family. They're self-sufficient." Or, she thought, if they're not they're jolly well going to be. And she looked a little grim. Aloud she explained, "It will take a few months to paint and paper the interior, with so much farm work to do. Then Mother will make slip covers and paint the furniture.

"Ross, I want to be proud of the place to which I invite your parents to come for our wedding."

Rosston paid the check with a thoughtful mood. When they reached the street and while they waited for a cab to come braking in, he remarked, "There are times, Linbel, when I think you care more about what Mother thinks of you than you do about me or what I think."

68

Closed in with him, she answered, "No, not that at all, Ross. You see, in my mind there is a rightness about things or there isn't. When we were high school kids we thought eloping was a lark. Now we realize our marriage wouldn't have lasted. Now don't argue — "

"You won't give me a chance — "

"It wouldn't have been your fault, but mine. I'd have felt inferior. I was an out and out Okie, in the slang conception of that term. I love my family, but I wouldn't have enjoyed having them visit me when your folks were around. We would all have been miserable."

"Meaning we'd married each other's families?"

"Doesn't every couple in the last analysis?" she asked reasonably. "And when children come along, they're descendants of both sides, and as I expect to have a dozen — "

"Gosh, Linbel, maybe I'd better switch to agriculture. I don't know that a budding bookkeeper can feed — "

"Oh, be sensible," she chided him. "I was speaking figuratively. And you'd better keep the cab if you expect to reach that lecture before it's over."

Ross took her to the apartment house door, asking how he could reach a lecture *after* it was over, then sobered and said he'd be up the next day about one o'clock; they'd go into things then.

They didn't. For all his light-hearted approach to serious matters, Rosston had a sense of responsibility as great as Linbel's.

Besides, Linbel looked 'delectable,' he insisted, in her pink house frock. And why should he plan a fourteen-room house when she could accomplish miracles in an apartment so small he'd have to wear long-sleeved underwear at the gym or else explain how he'd contracted so many black and blue spots?

"Places like these should have sliding doors, never any knobs," he informed her. And when she said she'd been thinking of adding a freezer, he asked if she meant to use it as a guest room or a clothes closet.

"I'm serious," she insisted. "I've an idea running around in the back of my mind. If it ever gets out in front, I'll be able to talk about it."

70

The Millers had a huge freezer on the farm, as well as a locker in town. "But the folks need it," Rosston explained. "It's easier on Mother than canning, and with a big family it's an economy, especially with so much of what goes into it grown on the place. On the other hand, cooking for one — "

"I wish you'd try it sometimes," Linbel flashed. "And don't tell me what I can buy in frozen foods. I know. But there must be an easier way." And back in her mind the thought persisted.

He couldn't stay too long, but each moment seemed the more precious because of this, and they made the most of their time: made and discarded plans, made and shelved plans.

"I'll run down to your folks' farm first time I have the chance," Rosston promised. "It's not as far from the campus as you'd think, by car."

His visit had been a delightful interlude in Linbel's work routine. Willingly she returned to it.

Everyone from Rob Mercer to the lowliest boy in the shipping department commented on the change in her appearance. The latter said, "Wow!" which at his age was tops in commendation. Mercer was more conservative.

Only the bookkeeper questioned the improvement. "How," he asked, "are you going to keep Miss Olivia liking you if you come in looking as pretty as she does?"

But Miss Olivia posed no immediate threat. As Linbel had surmised, once the girl had found someone agreeing with her, commending her idea, she was quite willing to put it off. She could talk about it in the interim; meanwhile she accepted an invitation to go to Honolulu on a long visit.

False spring came in sunny and cold. Letters from the farm were brief but indicated a heavy work program. The men were trying to do both fall and early winter work at the same time.

Linbel's mother wrote of her feeling about the house in lyric language. "It fair puts its arms about us, come night time," she confided by mail.

But Candy continued to be a problem. She was not being accepted at high school. Calvin wrote they'd told her it was the 'goo' she used on her face. Her father had thrown it away, but she'd bought more with her lunch money, and he'd given up.

A letter from Rosston arrived at the same time. He planned to visit 'your folks' the next weekend. In her reply Linbel poured out her concern over Candy.

Mrs. Lantz' next letter was a song of ecstasy.

'He done more in two days than you and your pa and me ever could do with the girl. He took her to some high school doings Saturday night, and when she came down lookin' like a circus clown he just walked over to her and began pulling things off — earrings and necklaces and bracelets.

'Then he told her did she go wash that goo off her face and eyelashes and comb the stuff outen her hair and leave it hang natural, she'd be prettier than a movie star. And she did.

'And when she introduced him to the other kids as her sister's boy-friend from college — well, like Cal said, she

73

done struck pay dirt. Now she's got lots o' friends and she don't go roun' lookin' fancy.'

A letter from Lanny, with a check enclosed, asked her to buy something nice for their mother to wear to his wedding. Rose was buying her dentures, and would she, 'for Pete's sake,' see that Candy didn't try to steal the show. Judy had asked her to be bridesmaid; Jan would be flower girl.

The Lantz family was really taking its place in the world, Linbel thought happily.

Mercer's was holding its own under Linbel's carefully thought out sales program of 'Budget Buying.' However, it was having a rather peculiar effect upon her. As each item was chosen for promotion, she literally projected herself into the role of Rosston's wife, studying what she would be most interested in at any particular season.

At times she felt completely relaxed, assured that not only would Mercer's ride the choppy waters, but that her family, each and every member, even

Candy, had found safe harbor.

With this in mind she shopped carefully, yet any shopping at all deleted the bank account.

It will build up again, she comforted herself the night she carried home a bargain in hand towels to be added to other linen. And by the time we're married — she shifted bundles to get the mail out of her box, then frowned. Calvert never wrote unless there was a vital reason for wasting time.

There was. 'It costs around a hundred dollars an acre to go into production, what with seed, fertilizer and sprays. Well, Dad didn't know about prices changing so much on house painting, and when Candy really bore down on him he give in. Instead of fifty to paint the house it cost five hundred; five acres worth, and now we're running short. Could you loan us some until harvest?'

6

LINBEL wasn't the least interested in food that night. The problem of food for one-alones was far from her mind. In fact, she didn't even care for the toast and the luxury of a fresh pot of coffee.

Just when she'd thought everything was going so well. Candy and Rob Mercer were two of a kind. They bought first and thought second. Only Candy hadn't actually bought; she had, as Calvin said, bore down on her father until he had given in, probably to keep peace in the family.

And her father hadn't asked the cost. He'd felt big ordering the place painted. And it was a big house; probably it had to be scraped and three coats put on, My goodness, he knew the rise in the cost of everything else.

Linbel went to a small file and brought out a map of the farm. Ten acres in orchard; fifteen in wood lot. They'd planned to plant that twenty to hay for the stock, and over here some alfalfa. There was a strawberry corner here. It would stand one more year of bearing before fresh plants were put into fresh soil some place else.

Now down here on the river bottom Calvert planned to put in cool weather crops, cabbage and cauliflower.

Over here went pole beans, and down there bush beans, and right here tomatoes, and way over there, corn.

Why, it was like a store with different departments, and up here at the farmhouse was the office.

"But what good is an office if the man at the head of it doesn't keep his finger on the pulse of the business?" she asked aloud. "Dad's having the house painted is like Rob buying those freezers."

Linbel brought out her bank book and studied the total left. And then she put it aside. "I'll never be able to marry Ross if this keeps on," she protested. And then she added, "How can I teach Dad to think first?"

There was only one way, and grimly

she set her lips as she answered her brother's letter.

'Dear Cal, I'm as sorry as you about Dad giving in to Candy. I'd like to help, but if I do how do I know Candy won't want a swimming pool and Dad give in to her to keep peace in the family?

'I think you'd better plant fewer acres this year and let him know why. Let him know those potential harvest dollars are all tied up in the paint on the house.

'And I think you'd better look at that cool weather crop twice before you tie up money in it. Those plants are all hand-set, and if you plant more than a few you're going to lose your profit in labor. Mostly they're planted down where big Oriental families work for free.'

She felt so selfish, so mean, by the time she'd finished the letter, she stamped and addressed it and hurried out to mail it before she could change her mind. After all, she owed Rosston something, too.

"And if I don't settle down and marry him, he's going to fiddle-faddle around and find another girl."

Later she allowed herself the luxury of a few tears. Now she'd never be able to buy a little old second-hand car as she'd planned. And she did want one to run down to the farm and to the campus.

She bought the car the next morning, and named it Three Acres. It was of good make but such an old model it could sell for three hundred. Yet it was in excellent condition, having belonged to an equally old man who, the salesman assured her, 'never got it out of a slow walk.'

Of course she could rationalize the purchase. Sometime during the night she had awakened and said aloud, "If the folks are going to keep that farm, it's up to me to take hold. Even after Ross and I are married, I'm going to have to keep a firm hand on things until Cal grows up enough to know the difference between wishes and crops."

When she parked the car behind the store she was hailed by the head of the warehouse. "Miss Lantz, Rob's going to have to do something about these freezers. We haven't room to store any of the heavy stuff we need."

Linbel took the worry into her office and looked at it from all angles. Moving and storing would mean that much additional expense, yet with people beginning to stir from winter lethargy and business stirring also, new stoves, hot water heaters and other bulky appliances had to be kept on hand.

Mercer had tried a 'trial flight' with the freezers: a full page advertisement in the leading newspapers.

Many had come but few had purchased, so few they barely paid for the advertisement.

"It's going to take a gimmick," Linbel said aloud, "and I'm fresh out of them." She wondered if she should have bought the car. They were expensive to run.

But it was good to be mobile again. She'd had the use of the Miller cars, and occasionally a truck, while she was there, and had kept up her driver's license. Now she decided to run down to the farm that weekend and check on the situation.

By starting at dawn she could reach there in midmorning. Linbel started at dawn, and when she came to the turn-out got blindly from her parked car and stood a moment before opening her eyes to look down on 'my father's farm.'

"Oh no," she cried when she did look, and whisked back in to go tearing into the driveway.

"It won't look so bad once the trees are leafed out," Mrs. Lantz comforted her, baring gleaming new white teeth. "And it was a sight bettern what Candy picked out first off. She'd seen a magazine cover, all yellow and pink, but your pa held out for one color. Of course it is a mite *too* pink. It'll fade."

It would, but not in time for her wedding, in the winter there would be no trees to hide that particularly virulent shade.

"Come 'long in," continued Mrs. Lantz. "We made changes here too, but this is my quarters. I'm not so easy got at as your pa."

The family was out picking strawberries. Soon now, Mrs. Lantz confided proudly, they'd be having 'cash money again.' They'd need it. They hadn't 'nowise figured on what livin' in a house costs.'

81

There was power and telephone and a dozen and one expenses that came as sure as the first of the month.

And Linbel worried. She hadn't thought of the family's inability to adjust to what had once been a familiar life. Too much had changed in the twenty years.

Lanny had postponed his wedding two weeks until the end of berry picking. He was a mite worried about his job. Business was only fair to middling, and he wondered should he take on a wife at such a time.

"I told him to go 'long and marry up," Mrs. Lantz reported. "I told him did the bottom fall out of the hole, he could come along here, him and his Judy, and live. We got us a big house, and I aim to put by every bite of food I can lay hand to."

"And, Mom," Linbel said seriously, "you see to it that Dad and Cal hang onto the money. Maybe you'd better freshen up on figuring and keep books, handle the cash. Dad will give in so's to feel big after so many years of feeling little. And Cal — well, if Cal thought he had an acre that needed powdered gold, he'd powder the gold to feed it."

"Meanin' we won't keep on havin' a roof do they spend the tax money. Lindabelle, there ain't never a let-up on economizin', is there? Well," she placed hands on her knees and straightened, "I've driven hoss sense into the two of them before; figure I can do it again."

The other members of the family came in at noon, hot and berry-stained, all glad to see Linbel, all trying to talk at the same time.

Linbel noticed a subtle change in Candy. She was house-proud, and that could be good. And she didn't mind picking for nothing; the rest of the high school kids did it for their folk.

Little Jan, who'd 'grown up between rows,' there having been no baby-sitters for migrant labor, had picked with zest that morning. Linbel offered to pick that afternoon.

"Daughter, if you'd as soon, I'd like you to take the load into the plant," began Mr. Lantz.

"Pa don't cotton to the fellows there," Calvert explained. "They act biggity."

"'Tain't that; they down-grade the load," defended his father. "They treat me like I don't know grading. I don't like cheats anywheres along the line. Now Lindabelle, she'll know how to stand up to them."

A little quiver of apprehension ran over Linbel. Her father must not quarrel with his only market. These men were probably only treating him as they treated lots of men with a south-western accent. Maybe that real estate agent had talked, belittled them or something.

Well, she'd straighten *that* out!

Candy wanted to go with her, but Linbel said there wouldn't be room. She was taking her mother in to buy a good foundation for the wedding. Mr. Lantz went out, shaking his head over the way women folk took on about marrying ceremonies.

What Linbel really wanted was to meet the men at the plant alone, to be alert to that peculiar sense she'd developed at Mercer's.

She almost wished she hadn't. The plant wasn't as large as many she'd seen. At the weighing station were two men, one of whom appeared to be a partner from his attitude.

Defiantly he down-graded the berries, and Linbel, knowing from experience the quality she was carrying, didn't flare up at him, though he waited.

"Why," she asked curiously, "are you doing this? Is it necessary?"

She saw the answer in his eyes before he recovered from his surprise. "Look, if you don't like our grading take your load somewheres else."

She accepted the grading and moved on thoughtfully and unhappily. In town she found her mother at a coffee shop, in deep conversation with a red-faced woman in jeans.

"I right out and told him what I thought o' his grading, and he told me to take my berries some place else, and I said if I did I'd take every doggone berry in the valley right along with me."

She stopped as Linbel came up, and her mother introduced her to this Mrs. Matheson, whom she'd met at the grange.

"Is there any other plant?" Linbel asked.

Mrs. Matheson shook her head. "And without contracts we'd lose our whole harvest this year. He knows it. He knows he's got us over a barrel."

"Isn't there a government inspector?"

"Only for the packing, though of course they check the scales for weights and measures. Other places there's no call for them."

As she waited for her coffee to cool a little, Linbel saw her wedding day receding. She'd been at fault in not checking outlets for their produce before letting the family buy the farm. Of course she'd known of the freezing plant, but she hadn't looked into its financial standing or buyer relationship.

"I suppose you could set up a co-op," murmured Linbel thoughtfully.

"Not in this valley. We're truck farmers, and it'd cost more than we can raise to get our perishables to market. Besides, we can't compete with the big growers."

Linbel drove her mother around the small town before they started back to the farm. Now that she'd been made aware of the situation, she could see signs of deterioration everywhere.

There were empty stores and empty houses and a listless, defeated look about the men lounging on curbs, their backs to parked cars.

Mrs. Lantz chatted happily. To her, having a good neighbor woman such as Mrs. Matheson was worth more than money in the bank; it was someone with whom she could sit down and discuss household problems and what one could do with the young folk. It was one of the finer attributes of that home she'd waited for so long.

Linbel listened with one ear until her mother said, "Miz Matheson says trouble here is, all the valley folk are too contented. They don't aim to make money; just want to live on a farm and grow their victuals."

The valley folk and a good percentage of the rest of the millions on earth would find that acceptable, thought Linbel.

That night the picking members of the family worked through to the long twilight, then tubbed and were asleep almost before they'd finished their evening meal. Yet they were up at the first light.

And Linbel, realizing how hard they were working, grew resentful toward the men at the freezer for their attitudes and actions.

"Dad," she mused, picking alongside him as the only means of having a private word, "watch that freezer outfit. Try to get a weekly settlement. There's something there — "

He stopped and looked at her. "You felt that, too, Lindabelle?"

"I'll check on their financial standing tomorrow."

"I don't know about that weekly settlement. They been payin' off by season; saves bookkeepin', they say. I'm right afraid, daughter, do I ask for money now I lose my market for all our berries, and the beans and corn. Cal's got a right smart of those in, and his tomato field's a sight to see."

Mrs. Matheson was right; the outfit did have the truck farmers in that valley, 'over a barrel.'

"I shouldn't have spent that three hundred on a car," she blurted.

"Now, daughter, you couldn't have pleasured us more."

88

She had to leave in mid-morning. She'd stop at the university town, though it was fifty miles out of her way, for dinner with Rosston, and reach the city by nightfall.

Mrs. Lantz loaded the car with early vegetables, leaf lettuce and radishes and young green onions, as well as a crate of berries, and Linbel, wondering what she'd do with such largesse, was about to protest when she saw the pride in her mother's glance.

Even the last look at the house was soothing. It might look like a spanked baby or a freshly broiled lobster, but if it kept Candy proudly within its walls, the color was worth it.

"Write me all about the wedding," she called back as she drove off.

When Rosston came to the river café where they'd planned to meet, she thought at first he was ill, he seemed so depressed. But later she decided he'd been studying too hard.

And as always, they both cheered up when they were together. In no time, though she hadn't planned it that way, she was telling him about the trouble her father was having marketing his first crop.

"Do you think these men are crooked?" he asked bluntly.

Linbel surprised herself by her anwser. "No, I don't, Ross. I think that man who talked to me was worried sick. Before he snapped out the down-grade, his eyes looked utterly miserable, as though he were ashamed, and," she added with dawning comprehension, "terribly afraid."

"Business," he muttered, then leaned across the table and took her hand. "Lin, how would you feel if I told you I'd have to put off marrying you for a little while?"

It was astonishing. Here she'd been postponing the date month by month, but for him to do it made her furious. Another girl? His folks? Well, she'd let the Millers see the Lantz family was as good as theirs any day.

"I haven't any job," he explained patiently. "That plywood mill closed down. We've been having bull sessions at our house. There isn't a fellow in our fraternity who has the assurance of earning enough through work to risk marrying."

He laughed a little then. "Imagine being out of a job before you've even got on it."

7

GRADUATION, thought Linbel wistfully, should be a time of joyous anticipation. Rosston Miller looked anything but joyous. She'd have to forget proper rest and her allergy to night driving and spend more time with him that day.

In his car, they drove up a highway along a river that came rushing down from the Cascades and parked on its bank to sit looking at mountains, drawing deep breaths of fir-scented air, and watching a water ousel skim along the water and dive head first into the rapids.

"Now if we could live like that," Ross murmured, "live off nature — "

"What? No washing machines, refrigerators, television sets and, above all, no deep freezers?" And back on her shoulders settled the Mercer Home Appliance Company.

"Linbel, we could live in one of the

tenant cottages. Dad would be glad to have me on the farm. Bud still has two years to go at State before he can be around to help. We'd have the two prime requisites, a roof and food."

"Physical requisites," she corrected him. "Spiritually, we'd be miserable. You don't like farming, and what a waste it would be of the years you've spent studying for a different career."

She talked then of her brother's coming marriage and his worries. And she told of her mother's solution.

Rosston would attend the wedding, which fell mid-week when Linbel couldn't leave her work.

"I'll represent us," he assured her.

When she was ready to start back, he stood beside her car a moment, frowning.

"We'll make out," she insisted, and he agreed.

"With you around, who could miss?" he asked.

She wondered the next morning when the bookkeeper brought her a monthly report to type in duplicate. Something was missing some place, and it seemed to be contract payments.

When Mercer had read them he reflected a few moments, then asked abruptly, "What would the old man have done?"

"Basically, decided which he'd rather have: a promise of future payment or used appliances cluttering up the floor. He'd have checked the current credit rating and, if he believed it advisable, refinanced."

"Ridiculous," declared Mason.

"It's what he did during the depression; he told me so," said Linbel. "He said big houses could make enemies by playing it on the line, but a small business like this was dependent upon good will."

Mason mumbled something about using the loss against capital gain, and Mercer mumbled back that at the rate they were going there wasn't going to be any gain to use it against. And heaven knew there wasn't any warehouse or floor space for repossessed appliances.

"On this refinancing — " He left this

open for Linbel to answer.

"Actually, it means reducing payments to something the holder can handle. But why don't you look it up in his old books? He kept them; he showed them to me."

"Well, I haven't time — " began Mason, and Linbel turned to Mercer.

"I'd like to. If Mr. Mason will take calls, I can use a few hours each day."

Mercer said all of her ideas had worked out thus far; there was no reason not to try this one.

Linbel spent one of the most interesting weeks of her entire business career. She saw life in many different guises. Each house became a book to her, and when the door was opened and she was invited in, each had a different story inside. But all had one theme in common: worry.

"The trouble with this generation," one dour mother-in-law informed her, "is that they don't cut the cloth to fit the pattern."

"Perhaps the cloth shrank after it had been cut," murmured Linbel.

The woman was on the defensive

instantly. "Well, I pay my way here. I wouldn't have come, but the doctor said one-alone never ate right. He told me that people living alone didn't live as long."

Linbel cautiously drew her out on that subject, then left for her next call, leaving behind a relieved young woman and a mollified older one.

One by one she made her calls, read her books and filed the contents back in her mind.

On only two of the fourteen long overdue accounts did she mark a repossess. Four were marked for observation and one marked for leniency, suspended payments.

She'd go after the next classification as soon as she caught up on her office work. Meanwhile Linbel spent her evenings trying to sort out the many ideas she was receiving every day; filing them away for future consideration.

Then there were letters. Rosston gave a hilarious account of how he'd been dragged in as best man at the last minute to attend Lanny; and Mrs. Lantz a glowing description of the first 'downright wedding' in the Lantz family for twenty years.

'The young uns are storing their stuff here,' she wrote, 'figurin' does Judy travel with Lanny, they can weekend here and save house rent.'

And Lanny, according to her father, spoke grimly of his future. His territory lay in the logging and mill districts. Men who'd counted on thick steaks and mammoth roasts to give them the energy for their work had no work and either no need or money for such meat consumption.

Linbel drew her first free breath the night her father wrote the strawberry crop had brought the first cash money. Not all that was due, but a portion, enough to 'wet the bottom of the bank bucket.' Cal, he wrote, was begging for some new equipment, but he was holding out against the bean crop.

She had twenty-four hours of relief, with even Mercer's sales picking up within that time; then the blow fell.

Landsdowne Lantz wired his daughter.

'Freezer plant closed. Bankruptcy. Bean crop ready. Valley desperate. Need market.'

Rob Mercer's hands closed on her shoulders, steadying her as she cried, "Ridiculous."

"Then it's not bad news?" he asked. "I thought for a moment there you were going to faint."

The news was bad enough; Linbel's reaction to it had been the ridiculous part. She'd looked up to see white stoves, white refrigerators, white cabinets for washers and dryers all marching off like so many milestones, and on each the words: 'marriage deferred.' She'd thought: Why, I'll be dead before I can be free to marry Ross.

"You'd better sit down." Mercer held her with one hand as he pulled her chair up with the other. "Down," he repeated, and obediently she sat.

"This wire — " She handed him the telegram, and he read it, frowning, not understanding.

She tried to explain, but he didn't understand at first. Then he drew up a chair and had her start over from the beginning.

She drew a quick map of the family's farm location, a valley deep in the mountains with no regular through train service, just a spur track which had once taken out logs and now provided one train a day for mail and supplies. And in this valley tons of perishable fruits and vegetables were just about ready for harvest, and there was no market.

"This freezer plant has been taking everything," she explained. "All the farmers have had to do is to grow the fine quality for which the valley's famous. Now, with the big season just starting, it has gone into bankruptcy."

"Oh well they can find another market," Mercer comforted her with the ease of the inexperienced.

"It isn't that easy," Linbel objected. "Haven't you noticed that different freezing and canning concerns advertise how quickly vegetables go into can or freezer? 'Two hours from field to can.'"

That he did remember; it was part of his training.

"Refrigerated cars or trucks," he said

brightly. "They would hold the produce until it reached a cannery or freezer."

"What cannery or freezer?" sighed Linbel. "Don't you know this is all worked on contract? Every operator contracts for his harvest in advance. In this way he can plan his handling, the number of employees — "

She stopped, seeing Mercer looking bewildered.

"Think of it this way. You have a cannery or a freezer plant. At capacity it can handle only so many tons of, say green beans. You plan capacity runs during the height of the season so your vegetables will receive the government's high grade rating and you the top price.

"This is something you can't leave to chance. Before your peak season is on, your field men have visited all sources, checked quality, contracted for yield. It's a protection both to you, the processer, and to the farmer.

"Unless a blight or some rare weather phenomenon has ruined crops, there isn't a processer in the State who hasn't already contracted for his entire season's run of all fruit, berries and vegetables."

"How about the open market, the produce houses channeling raw vegetables to stores and markets?"

Again Linbel sighed. "That's the catch. Our valley is two weeks late on everything. Produce houses are flooded and paying bottom prices."

All of this she had picked up from Mrs. Matheson as she railed against the plant for downgrading the strawberries. Surprisingly, it had remained vividly in her memory.

Mercer remarked that the valley must have some selling point.

"It has, or at least I think it has," Linbel answered. "I didn't go into it. The realtor who sold Dad the farm said there were glacial deposits in the soil which gave the produce something of the quality found in the Hunza Valley in Tibet. You know, that's the place Hilton is supposed to have used as the locale of his *Lost Horizon*."

"And Lowell Thomas visited and filmed it," agreed Mercer. "Girl, if that's true," his eyes were shining, "wouldn't I like to handle that promotion campaign."

She nodded, worry like a grey mantle settling over her spirits. "The timing's off. The emergency is right now. Evidently the freezer people didn't pay full price for the strawberry crop. The farmers are stuck with growing crops, and they average a hundred dollars an acre, you know. Dad planted only part of the land, and it's cost him a thousand dollars."

She didn't say, 'his last thousand dollars.'

Mercer was thoughtful, then pushed the telephone toward Linbel. "Call your folks. Find out exactly how much market stuff is available now and get an estimate of what is coming on; then I'll take you up to Oliver's. He knows all of the angles."

Fortunately Candy was home. Mr. Lantz avoided the telephone as he would the plague.

And Candy had the advantage of having visited practically every farm home in the valley during the emergency.

Linbel turned from talking to her to report conditions were worse than they'd thought. "A good percentage of the farmers borrowed on crop for seed, fertilizer and spraying. They stand to lose their farms."

"Isn't anybody doing anything?" asked Mercer.

Linbel shrugged. "They're having a meeting at the grange Saturday night to see what can be done." And then she shuddered. "Dad told them maybe I could do something," she confessed, and groaned.

"I suppose one of the government aid programs would be applicable here," offered Mercer.

"That would be like giving aspirin as a cure for appendicitis," flashed Linbel. "It might ease the pain temporarily but — "

"And of course the plant can be sold, or even run by whoever's appointed."

"I know, but in the meantime — "

"Beans are spoilin'. Come on; let's visit Oliver and learn if he can think of a market. He knows food problems as well as any man in this state."

Linbel found Mr. Oliver to be an egg-shaped man who tried to look stern by dint of special tailoring and especially designed eyeglasses. Another camouflage was his voice which barked.

"Now what's the trouble?" he barked after amenities were over. "Quickly now; I have an appointment."

Linbel found herself barking in return, and when she was through Mr. Oliver snapped, "Remarkable."

"What's so remarkable about that situation?" Even Mercer's voice had lost its suave tone.

"About the situation, nothing. Boiled down, it's oversupply. Can't afford to flood the market. I said remarkable because a young and very pretty girl gave me the facts in concise fashion."

"She has an automatic file in her head," Mercer said gravely. "You touch a key and out comes a report; sort of an IBM gadget attachment which can give a compil — "

"That will do. Olivia comes in tonight; suppose you're meeting her."

Mr. Oliver did try to help. He telephoned every commission house, then, with less hope, the head of every cannery and chain of canneries and, finally, the freezing plants.

Everywhere the story was the same. Their production had long ago been geared to farm products contracted for earlier. There was no point in taking on more snap beans (or any other vegetable) which would necessitate running their crews overtime, or hiring night crews for commodities that would take up storage space as they gambled on their sale.

Mercer said they were crazy, but Linbel knew they weren't. "Mr. Mercer," she said earnestly, "don't you know that a large percentage of processers own their own farms, or rent farms outright to cut down production costs? Why should they lose what they've gained by over-production?"

Mr. Oliver said he was sorry. He offered to do anything he could to help, but could see no solution other than the bankruptcy court appointing someone to continue to run the freezing plant until a sale could be made.

Back in the car, Mercer and Linbel sat for a moment watching traffic, watching business people stepping along, bumping into shoppers who dawdled. Linbel eyed one slim blond who slipped through the sidewalk congestion like water, never losing the tempo of her stride.

That was the way to do it, she mused: to stride right ahead, ignoring blockades. But how could she do that with tons and tons of beans, corn and tomatoes literally on her back?

"We'll save those blasted beans," muttered Mercer, "if we have to fill every freezer I bought in that cock-eyed deal I made last winter."

Linbel swung toward him. It was ridiculous. In the first place, there weren't enough freezers. But his remark had triggered a thought.

"Mr. Mercer, may I have tomorrow off to run down to the valley?"

"Miss Lantz," he returned in the same tone, "we'll both take the day off, and I'll run you down there myself."

"Oh, but Miss Oliver — "

"So we take her with us. Once in a while her father's daughter comes up with a good idea."

Maybe, but Linbel's spirits sank to a new low. Olivia Oliver and that spanked baby pink house simply did not go together.

8

THEY came down into the little town at high noon and for a few moments thought it completely deserted. Then they realized those dark shadows over the covered walks were groups of men loitering with the peculiar quietness of the unemployed.

The freezer plant had been the axis upon which the economy of the whole valley turned.

They hadn't stopped at the turn-out to look down on the farm; and now, as they headed along the dirt road which would lead them to it, Linbel began suffering the qualms she would ordinarily have suffered for the past twenty-four hours.

"Oh, charming," cried Olivia as they turned up the lane, and Linbel dared open her eyes.

The house was still what she called 'that horrible pink,' but the trees had leafed out and were throwing dappled shadows on the walls. Someone had taken the ancient willow furniture from the attic and enameled it white, placing it at strategic spots under the trees where a lawn grew sparsely.

At a small table, her apron full of green pods, sat Mrs. Lantz, who jumped up when she saw the car, clutching the filled apron to her.

"Well, now you all sit right here in the shade; it's cooler than the house," came the hospitable greeting. "Lindabelle, you run along in and make tea; there's ice in the box and a cake under cover. Oh, and ring the bell for the men folk."

And Linbel ran as ordered. Her mother looked downright beautiful, she thought as she scurried to the rear porch and struck the big iron bell that hung there. Candy must have chosen that cotton dress of grey, white-sprigged, with a flower pattern.

When she returned with a laden tray she found Olivia Oliver as busily shelling peas as Mrs. Lantz, the two of them chattering like magpies, Rob Mercer, a slightly bewildered look on his face, kept turning from one to the other as though he couldn't keep up with them.

Mr. Lantz, Cal and Candy appeared, with small Jan trotting in their wake; then, seeing the car of a stranger, went to the house to wash grime from their faces and sleek back their hair.

"Well, now, I'm right proud to meet you," Mr. Lantz said to Rob and Olivia, and Linbel wondered if such words, in such a sincere tone could be improved upon.

Cal was ill at ease until they started talking of the crisis in the valley, and then became voluble. And Candy sat in such whole-hearted admiration of pretty Olivia Oliver, she couldn't be offended by the girl's steady gaze.

As usual, the dark-eyed Jan inserted herself into Linbel's arm and stood like another dimension or an extension of Linbel; Linbel as she'd been at that age, round-eyed and serious.

Things were bad, Mr. Lantz informed them. Crops were about ready for harvest, and there was no place to dispose of them.

"They made a mistake when they converted the cannery into a freezer," he confided. "Seems there weren't the

109

proper outlets, and the storage space for the frozen goods wasn't big enough to hold them all. Now canned goods could have been warehoused. But it's too late to do anything at this date."

Cal said it was downright heartbreaking to see the fields of fine garden stuff going to waste. There had been talk of starting a cooperative, but nobody had enough money. The farms here were small, and while they'd done well several years ago, for some reason the men at the freezer had been down-grading them, and their profits weren't enough to 'lay much by.'

"Some of them stand to lose their homes," whispered Mrs. Lantz, and in the grey look she gave them they saw the reflected fear of many in the valley.

Nobody knew quite what had happened, Mr. Lantz told them.

"We figured we could somehow sell the same market the plant had been sellin', but when we went to the bank and told them that they said that was the trouble: that market was gone.

"Seems to me," he turned to Linbel, "what we lack down here is a head.

These farmers are just growers. They ain't never had call to figure out the business end. Another thing, they're all right scared some outsider'll come in and do them out of what they've got left. I told them you wouldn't, Lindabelle."

Rob and Olivia looked at Linbel, and she, feeling completely faint-hearted, had to pretend she could pull some rabbit out of some hat.

"I do have an idea," she admitted. Then she added hastily, "But I'm not sure it can be worked out, so don't build up any false hopes."

"Why can't it?" her father demanded.

"Principally time," she replied thoughtfully. "I don't know anything about bankruptcy. I don't know that my plan could be gotten under way in time to save the crops. Besides — " She stopped, appalled. Did she dare tell them how many thousands of dollars it would take?

"Dad, who knows all about the business end?"

"Where can we get in touch with the receiver?" Rob added.

"Figure they're all down to the bank

111

this afternoon. Bank holds a mortgage on the building. Us farmers will get what's left, if anything."

As one the three visitors arose.

"We'll try to see him," Linbel said.

"Y'all come back to supper," Mrs. Lantz pressed.

"I'm afraid we can't tonight, Moms," Linbel said softly. "We have to drive clear back. And, Dad, I won't be able to say anything yet. I have a hunch about this. Maybe something can be worked out. I'll call you or come back the moment I know."

Mr. Lantz looked at Rob Mercer and shrugged his shoulders. "She's not even letting me in on it," he confided, and then his chin lifted.

"Lindabelle's always been that way," he announced proudly. "But when she does speak, you can count on it."

The little town was hot under the afternoon sun. In the bank, Mercer identified the manager and became the spokesman, sometimes prompted by Linbel. Rob Mercer had an air about him bankers instantly respected.

"About the freezer plant, we would like

to know what disposition is being made of it."

Hope leaped into the official's eyes. This was a branch office, and he'd headed it for years, had made his home in the valley and become an integral part of it. The problems of his depositors were his own. He could retire soon, but there'd be no pleasure in retiring in a desolate valley.

He'd spent his early banking days in the central bank in the city and knew the Oliver name.

A receiver had been appointed, naturally, and was at the plant at the moment. He could give them more factual knowledge about the situation.

Linbel leaned forward. "What we want to know, first, is why. Why did the men running the plant have to go into bankruptcy They had a market; what happened to it?"

He could explain that.

"The Marion brothers were tied up with a wholesale deep freeze outfit in the city. They sold freezers filled with a year's supply of frozen foods. At first all went well; then, as the market became pretty

113

thoroughly saturated, the wholesalers found they were getting more freezers back than they were putting out.

"According to the contracts, a percentage of the payments was channeled back to this plant. And that was fine. However — "

Linbel spoke quickly. "That girl in the laundry room told me. There were people who'd buy these freezers full of food, then, when the food was gone, return the freezers."

"Exactly. And they tried to collect for food already consumed. Unfortunately the Marion brothers hadn't scanned the contract closely enough and didn't realize they had no legal redress until they took one case to court this winter.

"Actually the bankruptcy was the result of a cumulative series of events. The Marion boys converted the cannery to a freezing plant five years ago. For three years everything went along fine; they received top prices and prompt payments. Then business began to slacken in the sales area. But it took two years for the wholesale house to make a forced sale, and when they did, the new owners refused to stock the outgoing merchandise with frozen food."

"Then the Marion brothers made their initial mistake in not selling direct to the freezer distributor," commented Linbel. "And now they're left with dozens of small accounts — "

"With a lot more than dozens, and with no future market."

"Was it your idea to fill Rob's freezers and sell them?" Olivia asked curiously. "Because if it was, this shows what can happen — "

"It doesn't," murmured Linbel, and turned to ask another question. "Tell me how the payments were made on the frozen foods? Over how long a period of time?"

"Eighteen months."

"Eighteen months for a purported twelve months of frozen foods which could probably have been consumed in eight months. And that means people buying those freezers continued to pay for food they'd eaten ten months after the last of it had been consumed. One can hardly blame them for starting economizing right there."

"It was poor sales psychology," the banker admitted. "Incidentally, the Marion brothers weren't the only ones to suffer. The Two-Valley Meat company, which had provided the meat, has had to refinance to absorb their loss."

Linbel looked so radiant that the two men and Olivia Oliver stared in amazement. She managed to say, "My brother works for them," and immediately stood up.

"Come on," she ordered. "Let's visit the plant and find out how much the receiver wants for it."

9

OLIVIA was most vocal in her protests. "But, good gracious, Linbel," she even forgot the Miss Lantz, "what will you do with a freezer plant on your hands if you don't intend to try out that useless means of selling Rob's freezers?"

Rob asked a more practical question: "What are you going to use for money?"

"If I tell you before it's all worked out, you'll think I'm crazy. Oh, why didn't I telephone Rosston to meet us here?"

She explained about Rosston on the drive over to the plant. He'd studied business administration. He'd spent summers putting into practice what he'd studied winters.

"If he's that good, why isn't he working?" asked the always practical Olivia.

"Because the plywood mill went out of business before he started," Linbel replied. "Besides, he doesn't graduate until next week."

Olivia nodded. "You want him present because he'd understand what this receiver says better than any of the rest of us. Right?"

Linbel nodded. "Mr. Mercer knows all about sales promotion and you about home economy."

"And you?" asked Rob Mercer, pulling his car into the shade of trees beside the quiet plant.

She shook her head. "I guess how much a specialist in each is needed."

They ran into bad luck at the plant. The man appointed by the court as receiver had returned to the city. However, the engineer was eager to show them around.

To Rob and Olivia the interior meant very little. Linbel, who had worked at the Alderman plant, followed him step by step, eyes shining, questions hurtling out.

"It's a jim dandy," the engineer said. "Small, but it's handled everything this valley has put out. Trouble is, the business folded at the wrong time of the year."

Asked if he had any idea what the administrator would take for the place, the engineer said he had heard twenty thousand, and added, "Not that anybody'd pay it. I figure one of the big outfits will buy up the machinery and take it away. You see this valley doesn't produce enough to make a plant here worth-while for a man or outfit that could afford it."

"You mean their produce is too diversified," murmured Olivia. "Well, why can't they concentrate upon one crop, whatever grows best here?"

"Lay of the land," murmured Linbel right back at her. "Didn't you notice our farm? Half of it is river bottom, the other half shelved. Besides, after you've grown the same crops on the same land over a period of time, your land peters out. These farmers know that."

"Sorry your folks had to step right into this, Miss Lantz," the engineer said. "Rough on them the very first year."

"Maybe not," she returned, and added, "If I could find a thousand dollars in each farmer's pocket — "

"Five years ago you could have," the

119

man told her. "But right now they haven't got the extra and are sittin' on what they have got to see them through."

Olivia and Rob kept their silence until they had driven over the mountains and, in the first town of any size, stopped for dinner.

"When are you going to let us in on this?" Rob asked.

"You bought a thousand freezers — " Linbel began.

"Oh, Linbel," Olivia interrupted, "not after what the banker told us — "

Linbel presented both hands, palms up. "See what I mean? Until I have exactly the right words to describe a plan already worked out in detail, that's exactly what I'm going to hear from everyone."

"Meanwhile my television program and Rob's freezers can wait," came the petulant observation.

Linbel changed the subject after saying briefly that she wanted to consult with Rosston Miller and her brother Lanny. She found the food at this café excellent; didn't Miss Oliver agree?

"I suppose," Olivia said, a smile

removing some of the ungraciousness, "but in the Islands — " And she was off on her favorite subject of the moment.

Linbel brought her back later. She explained that when one lived alone and had to watch a budget, purchasing and preparing food became a bore.

"Why don't you think up some menus for one-alones?" she asked. "You could write a wonderful book on that. Just think of the business girls who'd buy it, and the widows and widowers who've given up their homes and moved to apartments. But of course you wouldn't know about that."

"About what?" flashed Olivia.

"Oh, coming home from work starved and having forgotten to shop. Scrambling together something to fill the inner vacancy and finding it tasteless; or having to wait for something to thaw out in the oven, maybe while you are hurrying for a date."

Olivia Oliver was beautiful. Linbel, watching her, had never found her prettier, though her eyes were narrowed and her cheeks flushed with anger.

"Oh?" she asked. "Well, something

tells me I have the answer to that one, or will have. Not that I'll try to take anyone's job from them, but — "

She lapsed into a pleased silence, and Linbel's lips quirked a little, while Rob looked from one to the other with masculine wonder at the female of the species.

He was even further puzzled when, after he had deposited Linbel at her apartment, Olivia raved about the girl. But then Rob had been walking around the car to Linbel's side when Olivia had asked one question and Linbel had nodded.

Olivia Oliver's friends were to say many things of her within the next few weeks. She had 'gone off her rocker.' She was 'obviously trying to impress Rob Mercer with her adaptability.' She was 'competing with that pretty little stenog of Mercer's.'

The masculine contingent wanted to know why she would move to a cheap apartment if it wasn't that she wanted to show 'old Bobbie' that she could live on the income he'd been reduced to.

The feminine contingent held out for

the blonde stenographer, and the Mercer Home Appliance Company was graced with many of the city's younger set, all of whom craned for a view of the blonde.

But the blonde girl had other things to do besides tend to the curious. A part time stenographer had been hired, and Linbel had started out on a survey of her own, with Rob's bemused blessing.

After catching up on her duties in the mornings, Linbel would spend the afternoons calling on widows and widowers. In the evenings she called on business girls.

It was easy enough to find names and addresses. She'd found her first widowers in the park, a chessboard on their knees. They'd given her a long list of one-aloners, and each one of those she'd called upon had added more.

The business girls were easily approached and enthusiastic. And they too gave her names and addresses.

Linbel finished the last page of her report on Friday evening, and too tired and hot to face her apartment, pulled up in a drive-in.

Beside her to the right was an open car

loaded with young couples; to the left a coupé with a couple her age. For a little while she sat indulging in a rare luxury, self-pity.

Wasn't she ever to have the normal life of girls like these — dinners and dances and theaters?

She groveled in self-pity all through her sandwich and cold drink; after she'd backed out and started for her apartment, using the river highway, right up to the moment she saw a peculiar silhouette.

Along the bank of the river trudged a family, father first, mother following, children of different ages strung out behind. All walked with that peculiar slumped over gait she knew so well. She'd walked that way at one time. Her folks still did, a little.

Impulsively she pulled up along the roadside to call out, "Where y'all headin'?"

At the sound of her voice the man swung toward her, his face brightening. "Well, ma'am, our car broke down back there a piece, an' I was aimin' t' take the kids and Ma to a feedin' place whilst I picked up some parts."

Linbel knew there was no restaurant

for miles along here and said so. "Why don't you come in with me, and we'll pick up parts? We can bring back some sandwiches to hold the kids over until you get the car fixed."

Obediently the rest of the family did a right-about and headed back for their car, while the man got in with Linbel, who told him her name.

"Landsdowne Lantz," he caroled. "Heard he up and bought him a farm."

There were thousands of migrant laborers in the west and southwest, but Linbel knew they had a *grapevine* that baffled the closely coordinated state police of those areas.

When she drove on home, after depositing the man, the sandwiches and the car parts with his family, Linbel felt cheered for herself and her family, unhappy about his and the many migrant labor families that were left.

Now everything she had done without — food, clothes, the good times other girls had — took on new value. Her family was safe; they owned their land.

"And if needs be," she whispered,

running her car into the apartment house garage, "I'll put off marrying Rosston for another year to pay the taxes and upkeep."

Her chin was set in a determined line as she rode up to her little cubicle to break down the survey into figures she could use as weapons.

Linbel's actions the next day seemed most unbusinesslike. Leaving the part-time stenographer on hand to take calls, she, Linbel, proceeded to have her hair 'done' and then went forth to buy clothes.

"And I must choose something that won't be out of style by my wedding next June." She gave a great sigh as she said this, realizing she had postponed her wedding date another few months.

She was going down for Rosston's graduation and forgiving herself for such dereliction of duty because, as she had written Rosston, it was important for her to meet the geologist who had made a survey of the Rockend Valley.

Linbel had dinner with Olivia Oliver at her small apartment that night, and before the evening was over looked upon

Rob's 'almost-fiancé' with new respect. Olivia had really been working.

"If I hadn't taken typing because nobody, but nobody, could read my writing, this would have had me whipped," she confessed.

As Linbel was leaving she allowed herself one observation. "I've a fair idea what you're up to, Linbel, but I can't for the life of me see how you're going to work out the financial end."

"Neither can I," admitted Linbel cheerfully, "but Rosston will be able to do that. He couldn't do what you're doing, and none of us could do what Mr. Mercer will be doing."

"Or what you're doing. Exactly where do you fit into this, Linbel?"

Linbel looked startled. "I really hadn't thought of that. It won't be important, once things are under way."

She enjoyed the drive down to the University town the next morning. Rosston met her and stood for a moment looking at her. "Girl, there's only one like you. I swear you're the only thing in the world that keeps my ego from collapsing. I must have something worth-while or you wouldn't stand by. And I must have some modicum of grey matter or I wouldn't have had sense enough to forego all curvacious coeds. In other words, I love you."

Linbel didn't mind meeting the staid professor. But when she had to face the Miller family *en masse* she shivered down to her neat slippers. They loved her in a patronizing fashion, but to them she was still the little Okie who'd worked as their hired girl.

"Of course," Mrs. Miller said thoughtfully as, the ceremonies over, the professor looked up Linbel and drew her aside for further conference, thus impressing the Millers, "there was something different about Linbel or I'd never have brought her right into the home."

The men of her family groaned, and her husband asked her to check back on the number of Linbels who'd been hired over the years of their married life. "Linbel," he reminded her, "was the only one with enough fortitude to come back a second and third year."

"Father, you know I've always treated my help like one of the family."

"You sure have, Mama," he agreed, "just like a poor relation. Now don't get your dander up," he added, intent upon Linbel and the professor in deep conversation.

Linbel was radiant, not because this particular dignitary had sought her out again but because of what he was telling her. He had, he said, wondered why no one had been far-sighted enough to publicize the full-flavored superiority of the valley farms' produce.

He told her he would prepare a 'paper' for her and was confident that Miss Parks, who knew nutrition from A to Z would assist him in a compilation of his findings. He could have it for her within a few days.

"We'll meet you in the valley next week," he promised, and she told him her family could "put them up."

The Millers were insistent that Linbel and Rosston come home to the farm. But Linbel said firmly she had business to attend to, and Rosston announced that Linbel's business offered such a challenge to him he didn't need any rest after the 'arduous final weeks' of study.

Linbel did have to suffer through dinner at a famous steak house but found it had its compensations. She could wonder why she had ever been afraid of Mrs. Miller's opinion, why it had been so important to her to meet her on anything like an equal economic footing.

Because of the delay, it was midnight when they reached Rockend, where even the four street lights had been turned off on the dot, to save the dwindling tax income of the town.

But there were lights on at the Lantz farm, and the big pink house blushed a rosy welcome. Linbel had never been so proud. The whole family was on hand; people of substance, she called them.

There was coffee, and whipped cream cake, and Linbel didn't mind Candy laughing and saying, "Ma makes it at the drop of company coming." And Mrs. Lantz smiled proudly and said they'd never know how she 'downright hankered after a free hand with cream the whole time they were fruit trampin'.'

No one had much sleep that night, and no one minded. As Mr. Lantz said, hot afternoons were made for catching up.

Linbel and Rosston went to the white table under the trees, and Mrs. Lantz, watching them shook her head at Candy. "Does beat all the way you modern youngsters court. Now your pa, when he was a-makin' up to me, body couldn'ta kept him with a table 'tween us."

In the letter she'd written him, Linbel had given Rosston a fair idea of her scheme. Now she went into further detail, and he listened, alert.

"It talks fine," Linbel finished, "but I can't see how we can swing it financially. Of course we'd have to borrow the money with which to buy, and to borrow we'd have to give more than the plant as security. We'd have to show there's a reasonable prospect of putting the whole scheme over."

There was no youthful mischief about Rosston Miller now; he listened with an intent expression, and when Linbel was through he was ready.

"I did a lot of study and research after your letter and came up with an idea. I didn't trust myself on it, so went to Acheson and had him go over my figures.

131

He thinks it will work. Here." And he drew from the brief case he'd brought with him a sheaf of papers.

Linbel was fascinated. Rosston had drawn a graph for the prospectus that brought produce from farms to freezer to storage to dispersement.

The point of dispersement was the hub, and from this radiated lines like the spokes of a giant wheel, interlocking with the first smaller wheel and with a second wheel which would, he believed, make contact with what he called "that ever-lovin' money that makes all wheels go round."

By noon Linbel had the whole etched on her mind, and when her father came up to give her a questioning look, she could say:

"Rob and Olivia, Lanny and the professor will be here tomorrow. I'll tell you everything then."

10

THE whole valley, declared Mrs. Lantz, put on its best bib and tucker for the great day. Mountains donned violet scarves; the earth tumbled wild roses along the hedgerows; and the sky tossed out just enough small white clouds to show up its startling blue.

But Mrs. Lantz wasn't happy. Not since she'd left her father's farm had she had so much to 'do with.' She'd baked all day Saturday; now she roasted hens, ham and turkey. In her lexicon, heaven was closely related to hospitality.

The fly in her amber was Lindabelle and her young man. Here it was the most beautiful late spring she'd seen since she was a girl, and did those two young ones go wandering off arm in arm? They did not. They sat with figures in front of them. They talked figures. Mrs. Lantz could have sworn there were no exciting dreams at night; just columns of figures marching across their pillows.

"Figure Lindabelle's had too much responsibility too young," she complained softly. "Made her serious-like. But that Ross boy, there's no counting for him. He's fun-lovin'; it shows right up in his face."

Lanny and his bride drove in, then Rob and Olivia, then the professor, and finally, much to their surprise, the receiver, appointed to handle the Marion Brother's bankruptcy claim.

"I was due in tomorrow; then one of your valley farmers told me something was up today. So I thought if I were not intruding, I'd sit in."

Mrs. Lantz was all for feeding her guests first, but Mr. Lantz vetoed that. "After you've fed a body, Mama," he objected kindly, "they can't nowise use their brains, they're that comfortable."

Flanked by Judy and Jan, she retreated to the kitchen, while the others gathered around the table, where Linbel automatically became spokesman.

She addressed Mr. Rutherford, the receiver, first. "We've tried to analyze the cause of the Marion brothers' failure," she began, "believing that would give us a working hypothesis. In other words, we would not make the same mistakes.

"They allowed themselves to become dependent upon another firm for the collection of money due them. And this due money was spread over a fantastically long period. Even had the customers contracting for the freezers paid, the brothers would have been paying out money for a second crop before money for the first crop came in.

"They were further handicapped by having separate contracts for food and for freezers. This allowed the freezer people, acting in the capacity of jobbers, to repossess their appliances and thus salvage some of the loss, without passing on any of this resale money to the men who had sold the perishable goods.

"This called for an excessive amount of capital, more than a business of this size warranted. When the recession began and people, having eaten the perishables, returned the freezers, it was the Marion brothers who suffered the full loss. Because of the way the contracts were drawn, they had no redress short of going to court, a costly procedure and under the circumstances not worth the outcome.

"When the freezer company sold out, the Marion brothers not only lost the little they might have squeezed out of customers; they also lost their market. And because the situation didn't become acute until after contracts were let for canneries and freezing plants, they had no chance of disposing of the valley farmers' harvest this year.

"Their only choice was bankruptcy."

Mr. Rutherford had nodded as Linbel made one point after another; now he spoke.

"Miss Lantz, you seem very positive in a negative way about the marketing potentialities. Why?"

"With crops in and the expense of seed, fertilizer and spraying already met, the first thing we tried to do was find a market. We were stopped for two reasons. First, even the commission markets were overstocked. The other outlets had contracted for peak loads the previous year, and in their spring check-up had found these contracts would be met.

"The other handicap was transportation. Even working as a group, these farmers could not get their comparatively small crops to market without investing in refrigerated trucks. Refrigerator cars on this spur track would be too costly, unless the food had been processed, frozen into less bulk."

Rutherford nodded agreement. "Yet you obviously have some plan. I concede that my ability to dispose of the Marion brothers' plant as a unit is practically nil because, as you say, the investment of that much money for the limited amount of diversified garden truck isn't worth it. Now how could you create a market under such a handicap?"

Linbel smiled at him. "Quality. Oh, I know the big farms have the very best quality, but here in the valley we have something more, something so rare that the only other western valley with it uses it in capsules sold as diet supplements. There, even the grass is cut and sold as tea."

Olivia gave a little gasp and cried, "Linbel, should you make this statement openly?"

Linbel nodded. "I think so. You mean if this information were to leak out, Mr. Rutherford could hold the plant and sell at a profit to the Marion brothers. But remember this. Except for a comparatively small lien or mortgage held by the bank, it is the farmers of the valley whose claims must be met.

"I think the farmers are going to approve of our plan of steady production and will be willing to accept part of their payment in stock in the company we will form."

"Good girl," murmured Rutherford. "You mean sort of a cooperative."

"No, not exactly. To use my mother's homely phrase, 'Too many cooks spoil the broth.' They would have a stockholder's vote, but the executives would hold the majority of the stock, at least until the firm was established and had been producing for a given length of time.

"It is my belief that without a head, the arms and legs flop around. The authority and the responsibility should be invested in the head."

"And you've chosen the head?"

Linbel smiled at him. "No, we haven't

138

anything to set it upon yet."

She gave him a brief idea of her plan, showed the graphs, the surveys, then waited for everything to be digested.

"Lindabelle," her father broke the murmured conversation, "how did a girl like you come up with this id*ee*?"

"Well, Pops, I got so tired of coming home nights to some little ole piddlin' spat of food, I began figurin' ways of changing things. I wanted to dine alone and enjoy it.

"Just about that time Mr. Mercer bought up those thousand freezers, and I got to worryin' about losin my job, should we have a bad season and have to close up.

"And just as I was carryin' these two loads, you sent that wire sayin' the freezer plant was closed."

"I don't know too much about food, Ma being such a good cook, but I knew Miss Oliver did. One day an elderly woman came in, and one of the salesmen made some remark, and Mr. Mercer said, 'Not enough protein in her diet, according to Olivia.'"

"So when Lanny's company was hurt

by the bankruptcy and he was out of a job, I knew we had another piece to fit into our puzzle. Lanny knew all about meat, from buying to cutting."

"The final piece went in and made the picture clear when I remembered Mr. Mercer telling Miss Oliver we couldn't have a successful television promotion show without a good sales idea."

"Then someone asked me why my father had bought in this particular valley, and I remembered the special quality of the vegetables. There was a terrific sales idea here."

Mr. Rutherford questioned her again. "Miss Lantz, you could probably save yourself a lot of trouble by selling this produce direct, without the expense of filling Mr. Mercer's freezers. Just use the Hunza background."

Linbel shook her head. "No, I think not. There would be sporadic buying, that's all. By tying it up to the freezer sales campaign and the Dine-Alone slogan, there would be a certainty of sale; a proof of the quality of Rockend valley produce. It would be almost forced sale in the beginning."

Lanny spoke up then. "Sis, what I can't see is what you're planning that isn't exactly what the Marion brothers used and went broke on."

Patiently she explained again, "We're not selling freezers full of food, Lanny, or even freezers. We are going to rent the freezers and service the food."

"I don't get that. Service the food? You sure don't mean the food goes with a rented freezer?" And then he said quickly, "Gosh, honey, people'll rent the freezer and put in food they've bought some place else."

"Not this time," she assured him. "In the first place, they won't want to. In the second, the cost of the food will be included in the rental of the freezer, unless they buy the freezer outright. And few of the people interested in this deal would want to. That's why this type of freezer hasn't sold."

Mr. Rutherford said then, "I assume you mean to have the company buying the plant buy the freezers as well. Miss Lantz, that's a most revolutionary idea. You realize, of course, what it is going to cost in labor to service those freezers with food weekly."

"Just delivery; they'll order from our stock."

"Apartment house dwellers move a lot; there's labor in moving the freezers."

"There can be," she conceded, "but I have an idea they will be re-rented rather than moved. And remember that I already have three hundred, nearly a third of those prospective users, signed up of their own accord. If they move, it is more than possible the incoming tenants will want the freezer left there. You see, in Dine-Alone, couples can double their orders."

And yes, she had a fair idea of what the initial outlay would be.

She seemed so calm, so assured, Mr. Rutherford made the assumption she already had the capital to start this astonishing venture. And she didn't tell him she hadn't looked for it yet.

"How about these frozen meals, coming out on plates?"

Olivia spoke then. "No, Mr. Rutherford, they're in package form. Our packaging costs will be higher, but we've proven it will be worth a few cents more to the users, because there will be no waste, no food that has to be thrown away by these one-alones."

"Tastes are so different," she explained, "with older people especially. Each can choose what he or she wants from the freezer stock in his own apartment, but once they have ordered, they must use it."

And then, with considerable pride, she drew forth a sheaf of papers. "Here is a month of menus worked out for one-alones."

Mr. Rutherford accepted the sheaf with fingers that almost wigwagged, "This is not my cup of tea," then leaned forward to study them.

A wind from the southwest came up over the mountain, swept down and set the maple leaves over the table to clapping.

Candy, sitting demurely back from the principals, saw Rosston Miller steal a glance at Olivia Oliver, and frowned. She scowled when Olivia returned the glance. I won't let them, she thought fiercely. Linbel's plumb wore out workin' for all of them, and they're — well, they can't!

Linbel *was* tired. She'd worked hard to reach this first plateau and wanted to rest a little.

Two men glanced at her with concern. One was her father. Working girls had vacations, didn't they? And he looked accusingly at Rob Mercer, who shook his head, baffled.

"Well, well, well," muttered Mr. Rutherford, "if such a pattern as this could be established, I'd move out of my hotel back into an apartment."

As they waited for an explanation, he continued, "I'm forced to be out of town so much I couldn't hire a man permanently. I tried cooking for myself, but I'd always forget something, or it would take too long.

"Now, with this service — oh, but it's out of the question. It can't be done. The cost of paper products are going up steadily; your packaging and labor would preclude any possibility of profit.

"Besides, take a person such as I, or a widower with children who had him out to dinner several times a week, or a woman who gadded about a lot, took off for weekends."

Olivia whisked out another paper. "I thought of that, also of the amount different classes of patrons could afford to pay. Now here is a week's menu for the pension class. Here's one for the social security plus annuity group, here for the little office girl, and here for the high-salaried business woman. And here for the class I identify as salesmen, the in-again-out-again."

"Why the difference in price?" Rutherford demanded.

"Basically protein costs, cuts of meat, and whether they have just fruit for desert, or fruit in pies."

"Pies?" inquired Mr. Lantz with interest. "We used to buy us a frozen pie now and again; they's already on the market."

"Whole pies are," Linbel explained. "A body alone can get awfully tired of one kind of pie when it's stretched out for six days. The pie looks pretty tired, too, by the time the last piece is reached. Olivia figured a two-piece pie that wasn't all crust."

"There are those packaging costs again," warned Rutherford.

Rob Mercer really spoke for the first time then, and everyone sat up at the authoritative tone in his voice. Linbel looked at him curiously. She'd have thought, had she not been able to see him, that it was his grandfather.

"You're all overlooking the two most important assets of this program," he told them; "first, the nutritional value of the food grown in this valley, and second, the stabilizing of the customers' food costs.

"Linbel learned in her survey, if you'll look at that report, that our potential customers are on fixed incomes. They know to the penny what their rent and utilities will cost. Thus far they haven't been able to gauge their food costs.

"The costs of these menus are worked out approximately. We've had to depend upon figures from the larger freezer plants. At that, our menus can supply nutritious balanced diets, above the average in flavor, at less than the same could be purchased fresh, because of the elimination of waste.

"I believe these live-alones are going to welcome fixed food costs which fit into their fixed incomes."

Rutherford conceded that. And Mrs. Lantz cried plaintively, "If y'all don't come in and have your dinner, the victuals will be plumb ruined."

11

LINBEL looked out on the beauty of the day — the sky intensely blue over the granite mountain, a few white clouds like the foam of wild syringa blossoms on the river bank.

And then she sighed deeply. It seemed she had never and never would have time to enjoy such things.

A figure in the background stirred, and Linbel saw Rob Mercer move from the shade of a maple. He seemed to look anxiously toward the house, and when he saw Linbel and Candy watching came up on the porch.

"Ross wanted to show Olivia the creek," he explained.

"It is beautiful down there, with minnows in the riffles, and tree shadows. Remember how we used to love bathing in such a place, Candy?"

"Hmph," grunted Candy, and turned away.

"Why don't you show me?" Rob suggested.

Linbel looked at him, and a warm protective sensation swept over her, the same feeling she'd had so often since he'd taken over the business. She couldn't count the times she'd insinuated herself between him and trouble.

All right, she'd just give Miss Olivia a taste of her own medicine. "I know a better place. Mind waiting till I change?"

A whispered conference with Candy, and Linbel hurried to her sister's room, reappearing in pink pedal pushers and a white blouse, white flatties and a pink ribbon tying back smooth hair that had somehow fluffed into curls.

"Come on," she cried and, taking the surprised Rob Mercer by the hand, raced up the hill.

He stopped once to remove his jacket, his tie, and to turn back the collar of his soft sports shirt, then caught up with her.

"Lindabelle, I didn't know you could be young," he laughed as she jumped over a log in the wood lot. "You're always so sedate."

149

"Now what would Mr. Mason say if I came down to the store like this and jumped over, say a freezer chest?"

It really wasn't humorous, but they finally sat on a log to consider it — the expression on Mason's face, the horror in his voice.

And then they looked around them. Through an aisle of trees they could see the farmhouse, the barns, and many of the neatly planted acres, mountains rising in a back drop behind.

"The Lantz domain," said Linbel softly.

"Ought to make you pretty proud. Your Dad told me you were responsible for it."

"Oh, but I wasn't. We all worked and saved, everybody in the family right down to little Jan."

"But would the others have stuck to it unless you'd held them to the vision? Do give yourself credit."

She sat silent, aware of a muted bird song, of the resinous scent of pines under the hot spring sun, and of this very good friend beside her. Finally she spoke.

"I was driving them for my own selfish

150

sake," she began. "I didn't once stop to think they might want to live a little as they went along. I just concentrated on a farm for father, but not really for him; just a background for myself.

"I pretended to myself that I wanted to assure them a comfortable middle age. It wasn't true at all. I had the world's worst inferiority complex. I wanted this farm to flash in the face of Rosston Miller's mother, to pay her back for calling me an Okie, a migrant laborer's daughter; for being shocked to find her son wanted to marry me."

"You two had planned to marry that long ago?" he asked curiously.

"In high school, though we'd started saving a little even before then."

"Then the two of you listened to his parents?" suggested Mercer.

"Oh no," replied Linbel honestly, "we listened to *me*. Of course Mrs. Miller didn't know I'd heard her but I had, and I was furious. Until then I'd thought if a person were clean and paid her bills, she was as good as anyone else."

Rob's head went back and his laugh rang out over the hill top. After a startled moment Linbel joined in.

"Why, it is funny, isn't it?" she said. "I'd never thought of it that way, but it is."

"Lindabelle, don't ever marry. I don't know how I'd run the business if I didn't have you around."

She considered this judiciously, head to one side, wind whipping through her curls, and then nodded. "Perhaps. If we can work this one-alone business out so I can face dinner for one without indigestion creeping up on me, I might settle for the role of the nation's most alert octogenarian stenographer. Meanwhile — " She jumped up.

"Meanwhile I hope Rutherford can keep his mind on his claim against the Marion brothers, with you looking as you do."

They raced down the hill, each feeling happily satisfied he'd cheered up the other, and came in, wind-blown and pink-cheeked, to find everyone else decorously settled around the table for another session.

Rosston looked pained, and Olivia's beautifully shaped eyebrows lifted clear to the cluster of black curls on her brow. Then she took the center of the stage.

Mr. Rutherford, who counted decimals, had asked Rosston where he could find economy in the individual purchase of frozen vegetables when the fresh were four to five cents cheaper by the pound, and Rosston had tossed the question to Olivia with a glance.

"Waste," she replied, and began quoting figures from a U.S. Department of Agriculture bulletin. "Take sweet corn. In a bushel which averages thirty-five pounds, there is twenty-one and three-fourths pounds of waste; in green beans that drops to three pounds in thirty. Beets are the highest in waste, one half, but I doubt if we will handle beets; not enough general use."

She also quoted the waste in poultry: four pounds of waste in a ten pound turkey; as much as one and two thirds to a live roasting chicken weighing over three and a half pounds.

And Rutherford swooped on her answers. "Ah, but we pay labor costs and packaging."

Linbel came back into control without

even considering she was taking over the reins.

"Here, Mr. Rutherford, are the costs per hundred pounds on everything our farmers grow. These are government statistics and carry the produce from the fields to the consumer."

"Bless my soul," murmured Mr. Rutherford as Linbel nodded at Rosston and he brought out a sheaf of papers clipped into a jacket. "But are these one-alones to be vegetarians?"

This time Linbel looked at her brother Lanny, and after a start he brought out a report he'd made, on the buying and handling of meat.

"And storing," he stressed.

It was late afternoon before Linbel reached the summation. Rob Mercer, watching her, thought she was like an orchestra leader, pointing to one section after another to come in on the melody with its particular part of the whole.

"And I suppose you have experienced plant men to call in," Rutherford remarked as she closed.

"The Marion brothers," Linbel said. "Oh, please, those young men felt worse about this than the farmers. I know they down-graded in a desperate effort to carry through the season."

She wanted to say they'd be salvaging more than the farmers' harvest and the plant; they'd be giving two young men and their families, residents of Rockend, a chance to regain self-confidence.

The Lantz family drifted away to chores and to the kitchen. They were all going to the Strawberry Festival at the grange hall.

Rob and Olivia went into conference with Rosston over certain tabulations, and Rutherford turned to Linbel.

"I suppose there is no need of my asking if you know how much money you'll need to launch this and where it will come from."

She let a smile answer that. She had no more idea than he, but she was blessed if she was going to let him know.

"If we deposit in escrow what you feel is necessary to meet all outstanding debts, except for the farmers, and I bring you waivers on these, how soon can you let me know what you demand?"

He said this was most irregular, and

Linbel agreed that it was. She said of course they could borrow the money, let him pay the farmers, then have the farmers return it, but that would be costly in time, effort and interest.

He coughed and sputtered a little, and then she smiled and said, all right, let him go ahead with his plans. It meant dismantling the freezer plant and selling equipment at a season when other freezer men were too busy to investigate and buy. At best, he would be able to offer only a small percent of each dollar on claims.

"I think even the bank would be lenient," she concluded, "because when the plant goes, the farmers' income which keeps the merchants operating goes, and both constitute the reason for there being a bank in Rockend."

"Miss Lantz," he begged earnestly, "where did you, a stenographer, learn these things?"

She'd picked them up here and there and stored them away in the filing cabinet of her mind, and when she needed them they popped out as though the need had touched some secret spring.

"Mr. Mercer's grandfather used to talk to me a great deal," she replied aloud. "He liked to reminisce, especially about depression days. I guess I have a good memory. Then, too, as you'll notice, everyone in our group is a specialist of one kind or another."

"I had noticed that," he conceded dryly.

What he didn't say, though she heard it as keenly as though he'd shouted, was, "Specialists but untried. Who'll put money on a team of unproven horses?"

Realization of the enormity of the problem of financing swept over her like a black cloud.

"We're fighting for time," she said, as Rutherford seemed to be waiting. "Bean picking will start in another ten to fourteen days. We can hardly hope to incorporate within that time, but we thought possibly, if you sat in, listened to us and recognized the potentials, you might agree to operate the plant for this harvest.

"Dad says the farmers would rather gamble on a company being formed than let their beans dry on the vine."

"They could salvage some, selling them as dry shell beans, and there'd be no problem of spoilage."

"Not these; they're the thick pod variety grown especially for freezing."

She turned to him in desperation. "Look, if I underwrite the cost of running the plant and paying off this bean harvest, will you operate that long?"

He told her what she already knew, that it wasn't a personal matter. He had to do what the courts demanded. However, with a market promised, he could allow an extension, providing he could find a freezer man to take over the plant.

He patted her arm as they parted, but she wasn't reassured. In fact, moving toward the house, she found herself sunk in the deepest gloom of her whole life.

Ahead, the big house, the raw pink already subdued by oxydization and the effect of trees shadowing the walls, stood as the great milestone in the life of the Lantz family. It was home. It was security. It was the dignity of self-respect.

And here she was looking upon it as collateral.

158

Mortgage! That word struck terror to people such as the Lantz seniors. City people might have their homes plastered with them and accept them as they did car payments or refrigerator contracts, but not country people like hers.

"Iffen y' own your own roof, nothin' can beat y' down."

Going up to the northeast bedroom her parents had set aside as her own, Linbel looked at it with concern. It was shining clean. Cal had taken time from his beloved farm work to paint the woodwork a gleaming white, and he'd put up a shelf wide enough to carry a clothes pole.

They'd found some old wall paper in the attic. It had a yellow background, white and brown daisies and was enough to paper two walls. The other two they'd washed with a yellow calcimine. Drapes for the two tall, narrow windows had been contrived of some equally ancient bedspreads.

From the north window Linbel looked down on the farmland, the orderly rows of beans and, farther on, the yellow green and less orderly rows of tomato plants. From the east she gazed up the orchards to the wood lot where she'd gone with Rob earlier.

Pine trees were silhouetted black against a sky streaked with apricot and gold.

Imagine having once had this and then losing it!

Not that they would, she reasoned. If the company were not formed, she'd find some way to pay off the mortgage that would see the farmers through the bean crop at least.

I'd take a night job, too, she thought, and I'd save more than ever. I'd meet the payments somehow.

Rob and Rosston appeared below, walking through the twilight, and Linbel gave a soft little cry.

"And I'll likely never get myself married."

Dressing for the Strawberry Festival, she thought of her talk with Rob on the hilltop. She'd admitted to him, and for the first time to herself, that she'd driven her folks for a selfish reason. Of course this time it was worth having saved and sacrificed through the years. At least she thought it was.

160

Now she realized they'd have been satisfied with a small acreage, a cottage, something costing a third of what this had cost in money; a fifth of what it had cost in years of hard work.

Stepping into a barrel hoop skirt her mother had made for the square dance out of a single cretonne drape, Linbel stood poised on one foot.

Rosston. She'd driven him too!

Come to think of it, he hadn't had the good time most fellows had at college because she'd been prodding him about the future. The future! Why could she never live in the present?

She had for a moment on the hilltop, and it had been like having the walls of a glass case dissolve. There'd been free, cool air that gave a sparkle to living, and she'd seen everything around her as real, not as related to something just ahead.

"I looked at that apricot tree down the hill and saw the fruit hanging like Christmas tree ornaments, and not once did I wonder how much profit it would bring," she whispered.

And she'd seen Rob Mercer, really, for the first time, not as a young man slightly dazed by the business of running an appliance store he didn't want, but as an individual.

Not as an employer or a promoter, but as a man.

And it had been breathtakingly exciting. Why couldn't life always be like this?

Olivia tapped at the door and came in, and Linbel was downright proud to have her see the room. Makeshift as it was, it had what Linbel called quality.

Olivia agreed. Bright-eyed, she listened as Linbel pointed out the results of her mother's ingenuity, and the girl who'd always had everything she wanted nodded.

"How lucky you are, Linbel. Imagine a mother caring enough to do all this extra work. Hasn't she a flair for color! I must tell her."

Olivia, all in white, sat down on a slipper chair and studied Linbel.

"You're worried about financing this, aren't you?" she asked abruptly. "Dad — "

"No." Linbel spoke quickly. "He's a wonderful businessman, Olivia, but he'd swoop it out of our hands, make it into something so big we'd be lost."

The dark curls bobbed in agreement. "Once I built a doll house. I was having such fun. I landscaped a little corner of the garden and set it there, and he came out and saw it. He meant well, I know, but the next day when I went out my doll house was gone and in its place was a beautiful playhouse, everything complete to the last spoon. I couldn't let him know how I felt. He'd have been so hurt, so incapable of understanding what I had been trying to do."

"If I just knew some young person with money to risk," mused Linbel.

"Linbel," cried Olivia, "I think I know just the person. She's not young in years. She is in outlook. Hold your breath for three more days and we'll know."

12

MR. and Mrs. Landsdowne Lantz said they'd never seen their Lindabelle so gay. Mr. Lantz said it was the pretty duds Ma had made for her, but Mrs. Lantz knew better. It was having young folks around.

Candy said it was a sight the way Olivia made up to Rosston, and her father chided her, "Miss Oliver's just makin' the young man feel t'home."

"Whose home?" demanded Candy pertly, and ducked away in time to miss the back of his hand.

The senior Lantz excused the two dancing together, so oblivious to everyone else in the hall. When they'd first come in, just as soon as they'd finished the pot luck supper, a group of farmers had asked Mr. Lantz to have his daughter come into the sewing room and talk to them.

Naturally, Mrs. Lantz insisted, it was up to Miss Oliver to take care of the two young men, and as Lindabelle had called for Mr. Mercer — well, the two young folks had started dancing and just hadn't got around to stopping.

Mr. Lantz did something about it. He rounded up the sons and daughters of farmer friends, and soon all four had more local partners than they could manage.

Linbel enjoyed the serious young men. She'd lived with her father and her brothers' love of the land and knew how important it was to them to be able to remain in the valley. That they couldn't do unless there was some means of selling what they raised.

They looked upon her as their agent, someone with supernatural powers, and it frightened her a little.

She was more frightened the next morning when a group of men called just after breakfast and asked to see her alone. One was Dick Marion, the man who'd scowled at her the day she'd driven the truck in to the plant.

She went to him, hand outstretched. "I'm so glad you came. I'd planned to look up you and your brother before I went back to town. Mr. Marion, if we can raise a quick loan to prevent the plant fixtures from being taken out and sold separately, would you handle the bean pack?"

"That's what we've come to talk about," began the spokesman. "Dick here talked to Rutherford last night. The fellow told him you figured to ask the boys to handle the plant if you could swing it, so we thought up a way to help.

"We got together and raised some money. It isn't much, but it's the sum the claims man said would do."

Linbel, who'd been standing, sat down. Before her the pink house shimmered, and, unashamed, she looked at the men with tears in her eyes.

"I've been trying to work up enough courage to ask the folks to mortgage *this*," she confessed.

They paid her the compliment of saying nothing for a moment; then Mr. Lantz spoke in a ragged voice. "I 'low we'da done it, daughter, this farm meanin' as much to you as it does to us."

The whole group broke into protest then. They were all in on this. They were none of them out to make a lot of money, just enough to keep on living in this valley of their choice.

Mr. Lantz listened, then drew out a large handkerchief and treated his nose in violent fashion. "Well, men, this here puts me in a bad way. I just don't have no money to put in the pot, 'thout I mortgage."

The spokesman had the right words. He said having such a forward-looking daughter was worth more to them at the moment than cold cash.

And an older man placed gentle salve on his pride. "Doubt there's a man anywhere payin' cash for his holdings could dig up enough the first season to make a showing. I know I rode on interest the first three years, and I didn't pay cash."

Linbel wanted to take the whole party into her arms; instead she said earnestly, "We will make out somehow, I promise."

Dick Marion remained behind to talk to Linbel. He confessed that giving up the plant was like giving up a member of the family.

"You're sure you and your brother

won't mind working for someone else in a place that you'd once owned?" she pressed.

He studied her a moment. "Who else? Way you have this set up, Miss Lantz, it looks as though we'll all be working for each other and those one-alones you plan to feed."

"As for Jim and me, we're good plant men. But we're like a lot of fellows with technical knowledge; we stop right there. Handling a deal like you've worked up takes special knowhow, executive ability. We didn't have it."

Linbel's party started home soon after that. They'd stop at the Millers' for dinner; then Rosston would go on with them, stopping with Rob Mercer while the deal was being consummated.

"We need you handy," Rob had told him.

Linbel dreaded the couple of hours they would spend there as an ordeal. She wasn't sure what her reception would be.

It was gracious. Mrs. Miller kissed her and talked with the others, one arm around about Linbel's waist. "It's like having a daughter come home," she told Olivia, adding, "She boarded here with us while she was in high school."

Rosston, overhearing, laughed. "Dress it up, Mom," he said affectionately.

Looking around, Linbel saw new furniture, new draperies, new rugs. Mrs. Miller dressed her house as she dressed herself, in the current fashion. Of course it was still the same old house in structure. Puzzled, Linbel studied it to find out why nothing appeared comfortable or at home.

She remembered how impressed she had been when she had first come to the Millers', the loving care she'd expended on each piece of furniture. To the gypsy she'd been, the home had been the epitome of all that was beautiful and luxurious.

Now with wiser vision she saw the pink farmhouse in the valley was the better place because it was authentic, except for its color; it wasn't trying to pretend to be what it wasn't and had never been.

That gave her a key to Mrs. Miller. She wondered why Rosston's mother felt the need of this pretense.

Impulsively Linbel jumped up and went to the kitchen where Mrs. Miller was trying frantically to impress the hired girl of the moment with the importance of serving properly.

"Here, let me," she said, and went to the drawer that always contained party aprons.

"Linbel, you can't," cried the distressed Mrs. Miller. "What will Miss Oliver think?"

"That I'm lending a hand here as she did at our farm." Linbel was tying an enormous organdy bow. "You see, when people have never had to impress anyone, they don't know they're being impressed. Actually you're cheating her by not letting her see this kitchen.

"Why don't you call her in and show her the efficient storage methods you learned through your Home Extension classes? She might pick up a few pointers."

She had the advantage for the first time in her relationship with Mrs. Miller, and it was a heady brew. Rosston, watching his mother's bewilderment, chuckled; Mr. Miller observed that Linbel had improved tremendously since she'd moved to the city; Rob Mercer said nothing but felt he was watching another petal unfurl in the life of his stenographer.

And Mrs. Miller had the greatest satisfaction of her life as the party started north. Instead of her former hired girl riding with her son, Miss Olivia Oliver suggested prettily that they switch partners on the last lap of their journey.

Linbel didn't know for the life of her whether Olivia was trying to make Rob jealous, whether she preferred Rosston's company, or whether the change was a whim of the moment.

Stopping for gas at the first small town Rob turned to her. "You don't mind Olivia's highhanded running off with your friend?" he asked.

Linbel faced him, her dark eyes starkly honest, "I do have a funny hurt," she confessed, "but I know I have it coming. You see, I used Rosston as I used my own family, to gain an end of my own."

"And those ends aren't good?" he derided.

"Maybe Rosston would have been happier with something less than I wanted for him. He'd have finished college sooner, been able and willing to take a less glamorous position than his education now demands of him. Oh, I think he's capable enough, but — "

They drove out of the gas station and into the sunset before Linbel found the right words.

"I should have let all of them find their own goal, whatever it was."

"Linbel," Rob asked curiously, "have you had the desire to get behind me and push? Influence me into making the Mercer Home Appliance one of the big stores in the city, and myself into a big merchant?"

"Oh, no," she cried, shocked, "never. I've thought it a downright shame anyone so big should be crammed down into a little ole hole he wouldn't ever fit. I almost up and told your grandpa that one day. Only I needed my job."

Mercer's roar could have stopped traffic. "I can see the old man booting you out the front door and throwing your pay check after you. Not even from you would he have taken any suggestion that the store wasn't the pinnacle of every man's ambition."

"We were a lot alike," sighed Linbel, and Mercer laughed again, then stopped. "At that, you are. With one exception. You've the vision to see your mistakes. As with Rosston. He'll be around again."

"Maybe," she sighed. "On the other hand, what man with gumption wants to have his whole life laid on the line for him, when there's another, prettier girl who admires him for himself?"

Linbel asked Rob to take her to her apartment rather than join the others at Olivia's home for a light supper.

"I'm that tired," she confessed, "and I have to be chipper tomorrow morning. Like as not that girl has everything fried. It wasn't fair to hand her so much work without someone besides Mason around. He confuses one when he starts explaining."

"But we're keeping her on," Mercer said severely. "You're going to be too busy executing to pound the typewriter."

She raised troubled eyes at that. "Vacation time equivalent. We can't

173

afford two stenographers. I've already had one week's vacation, in bits. Best vacation I've ever had," she added.

Mercer voiced an objection, but Linbel hurried into the apartment house and on to her tiny cubicle. How it had shrunken in the last few weeks. If everything, every plan made failed, could she ever fit back into it again?

As usual, there was nothing ready to eat, and after making a cup of instant coffee she sat brooding. She'd changed, and she didn't know that she approved the change.

She must try to get back into her old self again. Take this apartment. She would remember how big and wonderful it had seemed to her when she was finally able to rent more than a housekeeping room with a shared bath and leaky icebox, a cooler outside a window and her clothes hung lumpily behind a curtain.

Getting up to heat more water, she bumped against a cupboard and felt, as Rosston had when he'd visited her, that she'd have to explain away black and blue spots or watch the angles.

Rosston. She pictured him with Olivia, and of course Rob. She'd seen the Oliver home, and that was where Olivia was going tonight, instead of to a stuffy little apartment that kept one gasping for oxygen. They'd be sitting out on a terrace, the whole city spread out in light patterns below. Rosston would think that a proper setting for Olivia, a scintillating backdrop.

Well, it was her own fault. If she hadn't kept him so closely tied to her, he'd have gone out with college girls, and Olivia wouldn't have offered such a stunning contrast.

Rob would be watching them quietly. That was comforting. Just knowing he was around was tremendously so.

"Even if he did go whole-hog and buy up all those freezers," she grumbled. "If he hadn't, I'd never have been in this unholy mess."

She didn't sleep well, and when she reached the office and found Mason and the new stenographer baring their teeth at each other, she decided none of this was worth the nervous strain. She'd just up and walk out. But she couldn't go home, not without a solution to the farm problem.

Like getting a wild cat by the tail. She sighed. There's just no place to let go, without getting torn up.

Rob Mercer came in, and the store world straightened out on even keel. Rob soothed Mason and Linbel soothed the stenographer, Miss Cooley, so by the time Olivia telephoned, Linbel was free to leave.

"I've made an appointment with Miss Kate for us," Olivia caroled. "She's the one I mentioned who might back us. Keep your fingers crossed. We'll pick up you and Rob at twelve-thirty. Tell him, will you, Linbel?"

She went back to Mercer's office, relaying the message in such a sober tone he was puzzled.

"It will be a real break if we can interest her," he commented. "I've been trying to run down a few who have the money to see us through. There are several, but none of them would give us the free hand we need."

"I know," Linbel continued to speak soberly. "You may not like this, Miss

Olivia being your friend. But as much as I like her and as wonderful as she'll be in her particular department, I'm afraid she'll go overboard if she's the one who raises the capital."

Mercer nodded thoughtfully. "You don't think Ross, with his cash-register mind, can control her?"

The somberness dropped from Linbel. "Why, I believe he can, and better than either you or I." Then she slapped contrite hands over her lips. "I mean she's so used to you," she explained.

Mercer laughed at this, then briefed her on Miss Kate.

Miss Katheryn Delaney, he said, was the type of rich old woman mystery writers invariably picked for their first victim. But Miss Kate was too smart to become involved in any situations which would allow her to be victimized.

She'd been engaged to a young man before the First World War, but her family hadn't approved of him and her father had sent him packing when they tried to elope. He'd 'packed' to the nearest recruiting depot, been sent overseas with the first contingent and was among the first of the American casualties.

"Miss Kate spent the rest of her father's life getting even with him. Above all things, the senior Delaney wanted a grandson to carry on the Delaney enterprises. Miss Kate refused to marry, and as her father lived to a ripe old age, Miss Kate had to find an outlet for her energy. She took an interest in business, opposed her father and nearly drove him to the wall before he retired.

"She's a formidable old girl," Rob confided, "but I like her. She's honest. She's cut off all money grabbers by channeling her money into foundations. And still it comes in. She says she'll not leave a penny to any individual, because inherited money carries a curse with it, and she's not mad enough at anyone to curse them."

Linbel found a mental picture of this woman who could mean so much to the future of so many. She was so preoccupied with it she was hardly aware of Rosston giving up his seat beside Olivia to Rob and helping her in the car.

"Linbel," he whispered when they were under way, "you're not upset about anything, are you?"

"Hush," Linbel reproved him severely. "I'm trying to think."

"Well, of all the — well, all right!" Rosston barked, and was silent.

"Ross," Linbel began immediately, "how much has Olivia told this Miss Kate about our project?"

He stared at her a moment, then laughed, mostly at himself. He might have known Linbel wouldn't be jealous, not when she had her little old single-track mind on something else.

"She hasn't told her anything. Last night her father was home, and he questioned all three of us. He suggested we see Miss Delaney and I think must have talked to her before Olivia called for an appointment. Now what's wrong?" he asked.

"Nothing," she said untruthfully. Yet there was nothing she could really put into words, just a feeling that things were slipping out of her hands and that when they did, they'd crash.

"You're looking mighty pretty," Rosston

ventured. "New dress?"

Linbel nodded. So new the price tag might still be lurking on it some place. But she had to look, and what was more, feel fresh and efficient when she met Miss Kate. This brown sheer with sand-colored collar and cuffs matched the hat and the slippers she'd worn.

Miss Kate proved as formidable as Linbel had anticipated. She lived on the top floor of an apartment hotel on the crest, with a view in four directions which would have overpowered a weaker personality.

A large woman, she moved ponderously to a deep chair, waved the others to nearby seats and said, "We'll talk a few moments before we go to the dining room. Now, one at a time. What's this hare-brained scheme you've thought up, and why am I supposed to risk my money on it?"

Olivia began talking, floundered, turned first to one and then to the other for help. Linbel sat quietly by, listening, wondering if the project sounded as puerile to Miss Kate as it did to her.

Then she was brought up abruptly.

"You, Miss Lantz, suppose you begin at the beginning and make some sense out of this."

Slowly, aware of the importance of what she was about to say, Linbel did as she'd been ordered, began at the beginning.

13

BOTH Rosston and Olivia made feeble protesting motions as Linbel started talking. They would have told her Miss Kate was a businesswoman. She cared nothing for a little stenographer who'd come in on a stormy night and found nothing there for dinner.

Linbel didn't dwell on this except as a starting point. She went next to the number of persons living alone, the run-down on the survey she'd made; the survey the elder Mercer had made on freezer sales to apartment dwellers in their particular area.

And then she came to Rob Mercer's purchase of the specially built small units and his inability to sell them.

From there she jumped to the failure of the freezing plant at Rockend, the dilemma of the farmers, due to the flooded market, and the problem of transportation.

And then she told of the effect this

had had on her brother's job.

"Running down the reason for the failures, I found it was due to the freezer people selling perishables on time. The appliance could be repossessed, and the value of the perishables could be regained only through costly court action.

"That is where I got the idea of selling a food service on weekly or monthly payments, with Rob's freezers leased as part of that service."

Miss Kate nodded ponderously, then barked, "And just what makes you think half of the freezer people in the country won't horn in on your market once you've proven it successful?"

"There are only two valleys in the west like Rockend," she replied quickly, "and the other is operating as a growing center for food supplements. Rockend produce will offer the highly nutritional advantages no competitor could find in any presently known farming area."

She handed Miss Kate the report of the geologist and the nutritionists, whose names were well known to the older woman.

Miss Kate studied this briefly, then

began throwing questions, sharp questions, and to each Linbel gave a quiet answer.

And then the woman pounced.

"Well, young lady, granted all of this works out even half as well as you've anticipated, all things come to an end. People, being people, will turn to new fads. What then?"

"Oh, the Dine-Alone aspect is only the introduction, the promotion and selling point," Linbel replied. "The young Dine-Alones will marry; the old ones will peter out, go into rest homes, for instance. But I believe there will always be a percentage who'll take over where these leave off.

"Meanwhile Rockend foods will be offering a quality others want, couples and families and those alone who do not want the service."

"Humph!" said Miss Kate.

After a moment she poked a finger at Olivia Oliver. "Where does she come into this?"

"She's working out menus for Dine-Alones, living in a small apartment and trying them out. You do remember what she studied at college, don't you?"

Miss Kate's disapproval dissipated. She

beamed at a fellow rebel. "And this young fellow, who's much too handsome to have any brains. I suppose he's your super-salesman?"

Rosston blushed to the roots of the blond waves on his brow. "I couldn't sell whale oil to a starving Eskimo," he protested.

"When Ross was twelve," Linbel spoke hurriedly, "he began to take an interest in the way his father was running his grain ranch, finding ways and means of cutting expenses. He set up a bookkeeping system for his father when he was thirteen, one Mr. Miller is still using because no other has been half as good."

"He has a flair for business management."

"Hmm," mused Miss Kate. "I suppose your father expected you to take over the ranch when he retired?"

"He's satisfied now with my younger brother."

"And you, Rob? Happy in that package your grandfather handed you?"

"I haven't any choice, Miss Kate," Rob replied. "I have the family to think of you know. I'm afraid my only interest in this affair will be the freezer angle."

"Rubbish," snorted the old woman. "Your mother doesn't have to keep up that mausoleum. Sell it. I happen to know your sister wants to marry. Well, let her. What if she doesn't graduate from Miss Marston's? The world's full of girls who are happy though they never heard of that school. As for your brother, turn him loose on that store. He's a real Mercer.

"You do have a place for Rob in this Dine-Alone business, don't you?" she asked of Linbel.

Linbel looked aghast. "He *is* it," she cried. "He's the one who's given us all of our sales and personal relations programs. Without him to promote it — "

Miss Kate smiled grimly. "And now we come to you. I suppose you're chief cook and bottle washer."

Linbel blinked at that. "Oh no, I don't come in at all. I'm just the sort of go-between. I've known people on all sides and gotten them together. I was only trying to clear away certain things so I could be sure of my job at Mercer's. I'm a stenographer," she added.

Only Rob Mercer knew why Miss Kate's head went back and hearty laughter roared out.

"Well, Miss Stenographer who came home one stormy night and had to eat scraps, suppose we go down to lunch. Incidentally, if this Dine-Alone business comes into being, I plan to be a customer. I get so infernally sick of the food here. But like the rest of you Live-Alones, I find it doesn't pay to have my refrigerator littered up. And I won't have a full time maid. They fuss."

None of Miss Kate's party enjoyed the food served in the beautiful garden room of her apartment-hotel. Linbel should have been in sixth heaven at least. She wasn't. Not only had Miss Kate withheld one encouraging word, but Rosston had somehow escorted Olivia into the room and held her chair. Of course Rob Mercer had been more than attentive to her, but Linbel knew he was only being kind or, perhaps, saving his own face.

And then, just as dessert was served, Miss Kate asked, "Where is there a freezer plant I can visit? I'd like an idea of what goes on in the business."

"Alderman's," breathed Linbel. "Alderman Farms has its own plant, and I know people there. I've even worked in the plant. That valley is ahead of Rockend; they should be running the bean crops now."

"Farms?" puzzled Miss Kate.

"Yes, Mr. Alderman found the best way to insure the sale of crops was to preserve the perishables. First he had a cannery, and now a freezing plant. And he has his own farmland, three thousand acres either owned or rented."

"That's a lot of beans," muttered Miss Kate.

"Oh, its not all green beans. Only five hundred acres as a rule; then, say, eleven hundred in corn and the same in potatoes; two hundred in strawberries and — "

"Ah, diversified. Well, tell me, doesn't anyone grow green peas?"

Rockend Valley could but hadn't. They were a cool weather crop, as were cabbage and broccoli; the mid-valleys preferred crops with less hazards.

"But you mentioned tomatoes. I understand tomatoes refuse to be frozen."

"Whole," corrected Olivia. "They do freeze sliced. But we would do what the Rockend packers did — freeze tomato juice."

They planned a trip to Alderman Farms the next day, and Miss Kate announced they would make it a picnic. Olivia would provide the food, and she must cook and prepare every bit of it herself, "to see if she can be trusted," the old tartar announced.

"We'll have your father take us, and we'll stop at Champoeg for lunch. Time you youngsters were knowing something about the men and women who made this state. All right, then, on your way; I'll see you all tomorrow."

Olivia drove Rob and Linbel back to Mercer's. It was only natural that she should take Rosston on with her. He had no actual business at the appliance store, and Linbel agreed he could be helpful to Olivia in her shopping for the morrow.

It would have been easier had she found a great deal of work on her desk. There was none. The new stenographer was efficient. That added to Linbel's sense of defeat. In fact, she no longer had a desk to call her own.

Rob Mercer called her to his office, and when she went in and sat in the chair he indicated, he asked abruptly, "Feeling as though you'd built a juggernaut?"

Startled, she looked up to smile faintly. "You're too observing," she chided. Then quickly, "do you think Miss Kate will back us?"

"I don't know. But she's interested enough to investigate, and that's a good sign. Linbel," he spoke thoughtfully, "you heard what she said about my brother. Now I don't know where she got that. He's completely irresponsible. I wanted him to work this summer, and he told me I'd had my good time during vacation; I could let him do likewise. He won't come near the store."

"He would if he *weren't* interested," she flashed. "Do you suppose he resents that it was left to you?"

Rob was silent for a long time. "I can soon find out. I've never let the family know how I feel about this inheritance. I think I'm going to break down and talk to Rand tonight. Linbel," he looked at her, his eyes alive and excited as she'd never before seen them, "if he wants it I can be free after a while."

He asked if she had any idea what it meant to feel, from the time you were a kid in high school, that you were honor-bound to fulfill a destiny someone else had laid out for you. Promptly she compared him with Rosston. Ross had shaken off the shackles of the farm, only to find new ones placed there by herself.

Satisfied with her look of compassion, which he took for himself, Rob brightened and told her to take the rest of the afternoon off; she'd been 'going on this freezer deal for weeks.'

She left, but not to rest. She was like a machine, wound up and unable to stop until the final circuit had been run.

The little apartment was hot and stuffy, and after changing to a light cotton dress she went down to seek out a park bench and sit, idle and unhappy.

She tried to convince herself that the principal reason for her unhappiness was Miss Kate's involvement of Mr. Oliver. If he said, "thumbs down," then thumbs would be down in the case of every potential backer.

If Mr. Oliver approved the idea, he'd get into the business somehow. He'd make it bigger and better, just as he'd brought in a finished playhouse for Olivia, taking away her creative participation.

It was peculiar, but when she got down to analyzing the Dine-Alone plan, it wasn't a mere matter of food and freezers; it was a case of human beings finding outlets for their efforts, finding careers, finding markets.

She thought of the beautiful prospectus over which they'd all labored so many weeks. This night it would be in Mr. Oliver's hands, and he'd be trying to find flaws, seeking out something they'd overlooked.

For the first time the enormity of what she had done when she started the project struck her. Before this she had been concerned with seeing it through its formative era. Now there were dozens of people and thousands of dollars depending upon its success.

Her fear that Mr. Oliver might take over changed to hope that he would.

Better a finished doll house, paid for, than nothing at all.

Linbel's final and deepest moment of worry twisted her heart physically.

"Dad would try to make it up to them," she whispered. "He'd mortgage the farm to the hilt, or sell it. And we'd all be right back where we were ten years ago."

Her father would give the money to the other farmers, feeling his daughter had led them astray with her dreams. Lanny would be out of work; Candy would be back with that no-good crowd; little Jan would grow up a migrant; and she would be out of a job without even her dream of Rosston's love to sustain her.

Could she bear to live through the hours until Miss Kate and Mr. Oliver made up their minds?

14

LINBEL was surprised to find the sun shining the next morning. Not that it reached her apartment, but by twisting her neck a little she could look up the air shaft and see a broad band of yellow just below the roof line, a square of blue above.

Rob Mercer was at the store when Linbel reached there.

"Talked to my brother last night. Linbel, he lit up like a Christmas tree. Do you know that crazy kid's been taking mechanics and electrical engineering on the side? He had hopes of some day having such a business. He could contract for houses, installing every appliance as well as the wiring."

"When will he come in?" Linbel's final hope of holding her job went skittering.

"Right away. He'll work here this summer; then I'll keep an eye on the place next year until he's out of school. Of course the men here can do as much as I and more." He grinned at her. "They won't go buying carloads of freezers."

Well, maybe she'd be allowed to remain until spring.

Then a fresh thought assailed her. Here Rob Mercer had gone and cut the ground right out from under his feet because she, Linbel Lantz, had had a harebrained idea.

"Great Scott, sit down," Rob ordered. "You went as white as a sheet. Something wrong?"

She spread her hands out, appealing for understanding. "Rob, I get an idea. I sell it to so many people. Do you realize what I'll have done to dozens if this doesn't go through? You, giving up the store right when jobs are so hard to find — "

Mason coughed at the doorway, a cough that was a choking protest at what he saw: young Mr. Mercer with his arm around his stenographer.

"Glass of water," barked Mercer, and Mason skidded around to the nearest container.

He was all eyes when he returned,

slopping water. Miss Linbel did look green around the gills.

"It's all right," she assured them. "I guess I forgot to eat breakfast."

Mercer reached in his pocket, handed coins to Mason and nodded, and for a moment the bookkeeper stood in indignation. He was no errand boy. On the other hand, Miss Linbel was worth it.

Since the arrival of the twins, Mrs. Mason had become nutrition-conscious. Mason ordered Linbel's breakfast with an eye to nerve strain, though he couldn't remember which of the alphabet of vitamins was supposed to reduce that. Or was it minerals? Calcium, that was it. Calcium as in milk.

When Mr. Oliver's imposing car drew up before the Mercer Home Appliance Company, Miss Linbel Lantz was pink-cheeked and laughing. She didn't even mind being tucked in between the portly Mr. Oliver and the ponderous Miss Kate; as they explained, she was the smallest of the lot.

They had a gay time driving south. They went past the shores of a beautiful lake, with beautiful homes lining its shores. "Sucker Lake," barked Miss Kate. "Remind me to tell you about it later. It means something."

When they came to the wide Williamette Valley Linbel felt a personal pride in the farms that grew ever larger as they progressed south. She'd worked on so many of them.

In mid-morning they reached a little settlement that was the headquarters of Alderman Farms and eagerly she pointed out the different buildings and explained what they were, what they meant.

That big one there was the cafeteria, and the low one that looked like a charming bungalow was the administration building. Over there was the garage for equipment, and there the steam plant, and that big, big building was the freezer that housed everything from wind tunnel to laboratory.

Linbel took them first to the checkers' building, a veritable sentry station built alongside a weighing stand now occupied by a huge truck full of green beans.

"Be with you in a minute," called a slim girl in pedal pushers and pony tail, "soon as I check these in."

A handful of beans and she was inside. Linbel told them she was checking for beetle bite, rot, rust, wind rub, scab, rust and clusters.

"Clusters?" frowned Miss Kate.

"Takes extra handling," Linbel explained. "This culling of each load is the way they grade them during the weight check. Later you'll see more grading and culling until, after the river of beans has passed the final cleaning and is ready for packaging, there is an almost perfect if not perfect pack."

Linbel thought she could have told the characteristics of each member of her party by the questions he asked. Mr. Oliver wanted to know what tonnage was picked in a day, and Linbel replied seventy-five to eighty tons. Miss Kate wanted to know how the Alderman executives could gauge the number of help needed, and Belle Wood, the young woman checking, came out in time to answer.

That problem was solved in the winter as fields were planned. Rotation planting meant there was no overpowering peak season but steady employment for all from the field to the processing crews.

Olivia wanted to know about the beans proper, why they were graded in different sizes, and it was explained to her that they went into different packs, the oversize beans to be sliced for French cut; the other sizes for freezer compartments or grocers' shelves of canned goods, right down to the small cuts for soup.

Rosston, naturally, wanted to know about costs, and Mrs. Wood promised to turn him over to the man who could break these down as he wanted them.

As they were crossing to the freezer plant a school type bus with an Alderman Farms sign across the front drove in, and a motley crew descended.

Ordinarily, Mrs. Wood explained, they came in at dawn, as did most pickers. These were from the city's Skid Row.

"Sometimes weather takes production in her hands," Linbel offered, "and crops come on faster than regular crews can handle them. Then the busses go into the employment offices and bring out whoever is willing to work."

"And they work just long enough to earn a few dollars," Mrs. Wood offered, "then come in to the canteen for soft drinks and candy, saving enough for the inevitable bottle of wine when they're back in the city."

Rob Mercer looked from these men to Linbel, and Mrs. Wood was quick to catch his thought. "Pickers work in crews," she said quickly. "There are family groups and school groups from different small towns; many of the grade school children earn their winter clothes by helping with summer crops."

Rob smiled at Linbel, and she thought she saw a certain relief and understanding. She had not been thrown into company with such as these pathetic, shambling men.

"Our plant crews," Mrs. Wood was saying as they skirted a railroad spur track and went up on a loading platform, "are mostly drawn from nearby towns, housewives who find this a pleasant way to augment their husbands' salaries."

The truck of beans she'd checked was now backed up to a hopper, and beans were pouring into it and riding out in a thin stream to their first washing.

Following the stream into the big, light room where women in white caps and uniforms were working, Linbel had another sense of joyful homecoming. She'd been so proud of graduating from picker to packer; of working in the cool airy room rather than in the hot sun.

Now the stream had thinned to a single layer, and keen-eyed workers watched this stream and picked out any single bean pod not coming up to the quality demanded.

"How on earth can they spot them so quickly?" breathed Olivia, fascinated with the steady stream moving along the conveyor.

Hot water and cold, steam bath and more chilling, and on they moved to be trimmed and cut and passed on to package; the package running finally into labeling, and thence into the wind tunnel, then into the freezer proper.

Olivia was especially interested in the laboratory where the technician was making a final check of the frozen beans for quality control.

"They certainly don't leave anything to guesswork," observed Mr. Oliver.

"In the first place, this business was built upon assured quality. And of course that reputation couldn't be upheld if anyone along the line were allowed to grow careless. Besides that, a government inspector is in attendance literally to check the checkers."

The men were interested in the 'mechanics' corner,' a large room where replacements for all types of machinery were at hand, and men on hand who knew how to keep the machines at high efficiency level.

They stopped for a moment before the machines that would handle the corn, from husking to shaving it from the cob at exactly the right place to insure kernel without cob.

"The cobs go into ensilage for the Alderman beef," they were told.

Slightly dazed, they trooped back to the yards and, thanking their conductor, into the Oliver car.

"Too much to absorb at one time," he remarked, "but I guess our little boss here has been around enough to be able to give us answers to anything we think up."

"If I can't, I know where to find the answers," she assured him.

They drove on to the state capital, then to visit the igloo plant where meat was cut and wrapped and frozen. There, by appointment, they met Lanny, who was voluble in his enthusiasm.

"They not only cut, wrap and freeze to home requirements," he said; "they also have a woman food consultant who goes into the homes and shows the housewives how to pack their deep freeze for greatest convenience."

Olivia went off with the food consultant, Zelma Herrmann, to exchange ideas on food clinics and to confer on radio and television programs. Rosston became involved studying costs with the business manager. Miss Kate and Mr. Oliver were in deep conversation with the man who had started the project. And Rob and the promotion manager hibernated in an inner office.

Linbel sat alone digesting every scrap of conversation that came her way.

"Linbel, mind stepping in a minute?" This from Rob.

"Linny," Rosston called, "when you have a minute come in and look at this run-down on operation costs."

"Linbel, you must hear Mrs. Herrmann's ideas about sales service. She believes if the basic idea of any business is to better the lives of customers, it's bound to succeed. And do look at her recipe file and — "

"Miss Lantz," this from Mr. Oliver, "if you are free, would you come here a moment?"

By the time they headed north again, Linbel didn't know whether she was faint from hunger or dizzy from the ideas crammed into her mind by all of the others.

Suddenly, as they neared the log cabin, purportedly a replica of the early ones, though Oliver said it must have belonged to one of the rich relations, Miss Kate turned.

"I need some excitement to give me a new lease on life. What do you say to all of us going into this Dine-Alone business up to our hip boots?"

"You mean you — " breathed someone.

"We," corrected Mr. Oliver, "are quite satisfied with the soundness of your venture. We will provide the necessary financial . . . Rob, catch her," he broke off to roar as Linbel quietly slithered down on the log cabin step.

15

AS anyone could have told Linbel, there was no time for romance during the organizing of a company with so many co-relating branches.

Occasionally she lifted a weary head and looked around.

That ridiculous faint, she'd assured her anxious party, had been from sheer relief.

"I just didn't dare face those farmers, unless I were bringing them good news."

"Of course the days and nights you'd put in working on this had nothing to do with it," muttered Rob, "or the way you didn't eat properly."

She'd telephoned her father from the office the minute they reached the city, and for a moment was afraid he'd received the news as she had. Then she knew he'd taken time out to find the inevitable bandana and use it noisily to cover the tears in his voice.

"Daughter," he said earnestly, "I

vow we're a-goin' to have the biggest celebration ever, and you're to be the queen of it. Now you come right down."

She said she couldn't yet, and by the time they would be free the 'beans would be running.' Then she laughed hysterically at the thought of a green bean tearing along the farm road to the cannery on its own power.

"Hang up then, Lindabelle," Mr. Lantz ordered. "I'm goin' to blow a gasket 'less I spread the good word to the neighbor folk."

They'd had their celebration without any of the principals present. Each of those was deep in his or her particular job, enjoying the organizing of his department more than he would have enjoyed the big party given by the farmers for everyone in and around Rockend.

Linbel saw very little of Rosston. He was constantly with Mr. Oliver, and Linbel was thankful for that older man's interest in the company. Miss Kate had provided the larger percentage of the money only after being assured that Mr. Oliver would supervise the company's organization.

"Lin," Rosston said during one of their few meetings, "I've learned more in one week with Mr. O. than I learned my whole four years at college."

"Ah, but you wouldn't have learned that had you not had the knowledge you gained at college first," she countered, and he agreed.

"But you do understand why I spend so much time at the Olivers, don't you? He has to keep on with his own affairs most of the day; it's the evenings he gives to me. And of course Olivia is there most of the time."

Linbel had drawn a deep breath and plunged then. "Ross, I want to talk to you about Olivia."

"Not now," he cut her off sharply. "Look, hon, I have to keep my mind on business, not on you two fascinating gals. I'm going down to Rockend tomorrow; going to meet Rutherford there. After that, we begin to become a bonafide company.

"You know it's terrific, this taking intangibles and welding them into a whole."

And Linbel had sighed. "It's the first

time I ever heard fifty thousand dollars called an intangible."

Other things had happened to ease Linbel's feeling of separation from Ross. Since Rob's brother was in the store, Rob spent more time on the outside, working much of the time from his home and calling her there for consultation.

Changes were taking place there, too. There was no need to sell the big house; the city timed its street-building program perfectly. A freeway would soon send cars streaming along where the Mercer home had stood.

Linbel had felt instantly at ease with Mrs. Mercer. At their first meeting Mrs. Mercer had held her off and studied her searchingly. "So you're the little girl with the big brain. You don't look in the least formidable."

Now, on the eve of the first formal meeting of the company, Linbel closed her desk at the Mercer Home Appliance Company for the last time, wondering how and why she had been eased out without having been formally discharged.

She told each of the salesmen goodbye and talked for a few minutes with the men in the warehouse and with the truck drivers just coming in from their last haul of the day.

Mason caught her as she passed through the store. "You will take these papers up to the house, won't you?" he asked. "Right away? Rob wants them tonight."

Linbel nodded, saluted the stenographer who had grown from half to full time and was saluted rather superciliously in return, then went around for her car and drove off.

She'd given notice at the apartment house as soon as she realized what was taking place under the younger Mercer's management. She would pack tomorrow and move down to Rockend for a little while. She would help her mother with the summer canning, be generally useful around the farm.

Driving out toward the Mercer house, she thought how perfectly everyone had been taken care of. Her father and mother were happy with their new home and their neighbors; Cal was enthusiastic over the farmland under his capable hands; Candy, chameleon like, was wholesomely at one with her own age group in the valley, competing with other girls in domestic displays in the coming county fair; and of course little Jan was growing brighter as she felt the security of her parents.

There was Lanny, married, with a wonderful opportunity to use his particular knowledge in the new company.

Linbel found Mrs. Mercer in a welter of possessions. "Isn't this dreadful?" she cried. "But I can't call in professional packers; they don't know what I want to keep and what to get rid of. Neither do I, for that matter. At the moment I'd like to wave my hand and have everything but a few photographs vanish."

Linbel looked through the vista of rooms and shuddered. "Mrs. Mercer, if you can wait until tomorrow I can help you. Except for the furniture, we could move all the things you must keep to one room, the ones about which you're uncertain to another and the discards — "

"To the rest of the house," sighed Mrs. Mercer, then looked startled. "Tomorrow?"

"I'm through at the appliance company as of today. I'd intended to pack what I'd accumulated at the apartment in the morning, but there's no hurry."

Mrs. Mercer sat down rather suddenly. "This is sooner than I'd counted on. Linbel, why don't you go through the house now and see if there's anything you'd like to have?"

Linbel looked at various pieces of furniture, thought of them as replacements for the worn objects at the farmhouse, and sighed. If only she had a little extra money.

Two rooms away she caught a glimpse of a china closet, all glass but its mahogany back, top and legs.

"Mother would love that," she remarked wistfully. "I've seen her look at one or two in furniture store windows. It's about like the one she had to leave behind."

And for some reason she found herself telling Mrs. Mercer all about the Lantz hegira.

"Young lady," Mrs. Mercer stood up, "we're going to bring your mother here and let her choose what she wants, what reminds her of what she left behind. Now don't argue. All of this is a burden to me now, yet I still care enough about what it meant not to want it to be misused by strangers. I would feel I'd found a home for pets. And we can have the boys carry it down to your farm in one of the company trucks.

"Now then, Rob will be along any minute. After your meeting tonight, if it isn't too late, you two come back and we'll have a long talk about possessions."

Linbel both dreaded and looked forward to that night's meeting. It would be the consummation of weeks of work. And it would be held in the offices of a refrigerated warehouse they'd rented to handle the stocking of Rockend produce.

Rob drove a silent Linbel across town to the big building. He reported that the paint in the offices was dry, and that the filing cabinets containing the new company's papers had been moved over from Mercer's.

He'd been lucky. He was able to buy a good half-hour on Channel X for Olivia's program. They'd debut the first of August, not too far in advance of the date they'd be ready to service the

Dine-Alone packets. Of course she knew he'd sold Mercer's for the price of the freezers; they were now all his, or rather his stock in the new company.

He had a newspaper advertising tie-in with the TV program about setup, didn't want to release it until they were sure of the contracts with the fisheries and the cool crop vegetables. He'd have those by next week.

Of course Miss Kate was riding on Cloud Thirteen; Linbel had to laugh a little at any cloud being able to float the portly Miss Kate.

The main office of the Rockend Dine-Alone Company had been turned into a board room; a table of planks and sawhorses were set up and disguised by adroit covering.

Miss Kate patted the chair to the right of her; her attorney was on the left. At the opposite end of the table sat Mr. Oliver with his attorney and Rosston. Lanny came by to drop a kiss on her head, and Judy squeezed her hand. Judy was to be the *firm's* private secretary. Mr. Rutherford, talking to a happy Olivia, saluted her, and Olivia beamed at her.

And then when Rob had seated himself beside Olivia, Mr. Oliver cleared his throat and the meeting began.

Linbel listened bemused unless called upon for data, which she was ready to give quickly and concisely or able to produce from brief case or file.

Everyone had bought an interest in the company in one way or another, except the attorneys and Mr. Rutherford. Mr. Oliver had bought shares for Olivia. The Millers had come through handsomely for Rosston. Rob of course had the equivalent of the freezers. Judy had borrowed money from an affluent uncle for herself and Lanny. The farmers of Rockend had gotten together to purchase a small block. Only Linbel had had nothing to offer.

Miss Kate, who had provided nearly three quarters of the money, patted Linbel's hand as Linbel smiled to herself. It was like the farm. She'd started the whole thing and then been left out.

Someone prodded her, and she brushed her thoughts aside. Mr. Oliver was saying something to her. Oh, he was asking her to take his chair.

"But I — " she began.

"Run along," ordered Miss Kate. "Where do you suppose any of us would have been without your executive direction? You first conceived the idea, worked out the programs for the different branches, chose your specialists and put them to work gathering details, then coalesced the whole into a smoothly working unit."

And Mr. Oliver said pompously, "Our managing director, Miss Lindabelle Lantz."

Later they took her to her office. She felt a little hysterical. She had planned the arrangements, chosen the furniture, decided where the lights should be placed.

She hadn't planned the neat lettering on the frosted door panel.

Ten weeks later Miss Lantz, managing director of the frozen beehive, Rockend Dine-Alone, handed a graph to the head of the packaging department.

"Try it out. Believe me, live-alones will appreciate a package of meat done in compartments. It's so difficult to cut through a solid slab."

When he left, she stretched, yawned

and dropped her head on the desk. In an hour she would start south. She was so tired. She hadn't even had time to move to another apartment in these last weeks. Well, her era in that stuffy little two-by-four was almost at an end.

Flowers . . . she did hope Rosston would remember to stop in Eugene and pick them up. Oh, but he would. After all he'd lived there four years. And the ring . . . But Rob would see to that. The best man usually did, didn't he?

Mr. Oliver had offered to drive her down with Miss Kate, but Linbel had wanted to go in her own shabby little car. She needed to be alone, to recapitulate romance, she thought.

She left last-minute instructions with department heads. The stenographer in the general office reported Judy had gone on an hour ago. And then she was on her way. If she hurried she would be there in time for sunset.

Linbel saw little of the autumn beauty as she sped down the valley. She was thinking of that night after she had been named managing director. Rosston had insisted on taking her home because he wanted to talk to her, now that they dared lift their minds from business.

It was astonishing how mental cobwebs could be cleared away by frank and honest discussions. Actually, Linbel had done much of the talking.

Her mind skipped to the farmhouse, the scene of tomorrow's wedding. Mrs. Mercer had insisted upon giving Mrs. Lantz the furniture she so admired and had finally grudgingly accepted some money for it, first calling in a used furniture dealer for an estimate so Mrs. Lantz could see how little she would receive on the market.

The farmhouse was wearing that furniture proudly. And Mrs. Lantz had even become reconciled to an electric range, refrigerator, deep freeze, automatic washer and dryer. Not that she'd given up her older appliances; these she moved to the summer kitchen. "A body can't never tell when the juice will give out. Come a storm and the power lines go down, we'll carry on like as always."

The sun was just topping the hills when Linbel stopped on the ledge above the farm and looked down. It was amazing really, but the red gold maples actually glorified the pink of the farmhouse. It sat like a glowing pink gem encircled by topaz.

Something moved in the chicken yard, and Linbel shook her head and looked again. Mrs. Mercer, a housedress lifted in front like an apron, was scattering grain. And then Linbel really craned her neck. Coming out of the hen house was Mrs. Miller. Thank goodness she was learning that quality was an inside condition, not an outside mode of dress or manner.

Rob Mercer was at the gate. "Been watching for you," he told her soberly. "Why not run your car in there and come up on the hill with me?"

She parked the car, and together they went up to the pine grove at the summit. For a moment Linbel stood there looking down on the little valley that meant so much to so many. Then memories of another day when she and Rob had come up here came back.

"Lin," Rob squared her around and looked at her earnestly, "how about this business tomorrow? I feel responsible, you know."

"You do? How, why?" she asked in astonishment.

"I'd always meant to marry Olivia some day. And then I couldn't — "

"Because of the way she seemed to fall in love with Ross?"

"Before she ever knew a Rosston Miller existed, way back in the late winter, one stormy day. Can't tell you the date or why, but I came in from the storm, and you looked up so starry-eyed I knew no Olivia could ever fill your place."

Linbel's mind flashed back. She recalled how she had looked that day — hair skinned back, threadbare blouse and the light sweater she wore in the office.

"I could have kept Olivia out of your life. I didn't. Because I wanted to be with you, used her as an excuse and now she's marrying your fiancé."

"Oh, that." Linbel's eyes were starry enough now. "He wasn't really. He was just someone whose life I was trying to run. Of course neither of us knew it until he met Olivia and found out what real love was like. Anyway, I told him the truth that night our Dine-Alone really came into operation."

"So that's why Olivia had enough nerve to ask to have her wedding here. You really meant it, and she, being a woman, would know."

"Umhum, she knew sooner than I did, in fact. But then I'd made a habit of Rosston, a habit of the idea of marrying him just as soon as I could show his mother my family was every bit as good as hers. Which of course made me as much of a snob as she was, but I didn't see it then."

"And now you know why she felt as she did?"

Linbel laughed aloud. "Yes. Ross found out and told me. He met someone who'd known his maternal grandfather. It seems that Mrs. Miller's people were real hillbillies. Ross was delighted."

"And my grandfather was an immigrant who started out as a shoe-shine boy. Linbel, I'm not much better off, financially. At the moment I'm worth one thousand freezers, eight hundred of which are in operation. If anything happened to Dine-Alone, that would be all I'd have."

"At least you could eat frozen foods," she teased. "Or no, you couldn't; the freezers belong to the company. You're safe as long as the company is, and when it isn't we can all come back and live off the land."

"We, as in you and I? Lin, you've been the executive in my life."

Slowly she shook her head. "No, you're the one person I couldn't boss. You were always one move ahead. And oh, Rob, what a relief that's been. I've thought I was physically tired. I wasn't. It was just carrying the responsibility for so many. That's why I've been slipping more and more of my work onto your desk, getting you ready to take over."

He took over then. The sky behind the pines turned gold and then apricot.

Down at the farmhouse, the wedding party waited until Mr. Lantz, after a little reconnoitering trip, came back to say happily, "They's a spring up on that hill. Bein's we got us a houseful here, figure we could build a cabin there by cuttin' a few trees. Give them a home place."

"But, Pa," wailed Candy, not understanding, "I'm hungry. How long do we have to wait dinner? I'm being bridesmaid tomorrow, remember, and I've got to do my hair tonight."

"Figure we can draw up to the table now, daughter. Don't believe them young uns on the hill will know do they or don't they have victuals."

However, October nights carry the threat of frost even in the early hours, and Rob and Linbel came down to blink at the lamplight and the excited faces around the big table.

Rosston took over. "I think we can catch the County Clerk in the morning, Rob."

"Daughter," Mrs. Lantz said softly, "I still got my weddin' dress; you're slim enough to wear it. I can do it up fresh come morning."

Mrs. Mercer got up and came over to Linbel and, when her arms were about her, said, "Daughter, I nearly told you that night when we talked furniture. That's why I asked you to choose what you'd like to have. I thought Rob had told you what I knew weeks before: that he loved you."

Linbel shook her head. "Cobbler's child. Our promotion manager didn't

223

say a word until this evening."

Lanny teased her. "And you, an executive, couldn't work him into a proposal? You, who've run all of our live — "

"If you don't mind, I'm through running anyone's life. For a change," she leaned against Rob's shoulder, "I'm letting Rob take over the management of mine."

THE END

FATAL RING OF LIGHT
Helen Eastwood

Katy's brother was supposed to have died in 1897 but a scrawled note in his handwriting showed July 1899. What had happened to him in those two years? Katy was determined to help him.

NIGHT ACTION
Alan Evans

Captain David Brent sails at dead of night to the German occupied Normandy town of St. Jean on a mission which will stretch loyalty and ingenuity to its limits, and beyond.

A MURDER TOO MANY
Elizabeth Ferrars

Many, including the murdered man's widow, believed the wrong man had been convicted. The further murder of a key witness in the earlier case convinced Basnett that the seemingly unrelated deaths were linked.

THE WILDERNESS WALK
Sheila Bishop

Stifling unpleasant memories of a misbegotten romance in Cleave with Lord Francis Aubrey, Lavinia goes on holiday there with her sister. The two women are thrust into a romantic intrigue involving none other than Lord Francis.

THE RELUCTANT GUEST
Rosalind Brett

Ann Calvert went to spend a month on a South African farm with Theo Borland and his sister. They both proved to be different from her first idea of them, and there was Storr Peterson — the most disturbing man she had ever met.

ONE ENCHANTED SUMMER
Anne Tedlock Brooks

A tale of mystery and romance and a girl who found both during one enchanted summer.

CLOUD OVER MALVERTON
Nancy Buckingham

Dulcie soon realises that something is seriously wrong at Malverton, and when violence strikes she is horrified to find herself under suspicion of murder.

AFTER THOUGHTS
Max Bygraves

The Cockney entertainer tells stories of his East End childhood, of his RAF days, and his post-war showbusiness successes and friendships with fellow comedians.

MOONLIGHT AND MARCH ROSES
D. Y. Cameron

Lynn's search to trace a missing girl takes her to Spain, where she meets Clive Hendon. While untangling the situation, she untangles her emotions and decides on her own future.

NURSE ALICE IN LOVE
Theresa Charles

Accepting the post of nurse to little Fernie Sherrod, Alice Everton could not guess at the romance, suspense and danger which lay ahead at the Sherrod's isolated estate.

POIROT INVESTIGATES
Agatha Christie

Two things bind these eleven stories together — the brilliance and uncanny skill of the diminutive Belgian detective, and the stupidity of his Watson-like partner, Captain Hastings.

LET LOOSE THE TIGERS
Josephine Cox

Queenie promised to find the long-lost son of the frail, elderly murderess, Hannah Jason. But her enquiries threatened to unlock the cage where crucial secrets had long been held captive.

THE TWILIGHT MAN
Frank Gruber

Jim Rand lives alone in the California desert awaiting death. Into his hermit existence comes a teenage girl who blows both his past and his brief future wide open.

DOG IN THE DARK
Gerald Hammond

Jim Cunningham breeds and trains gun dogs, and his antagonism towards the devotees of show spaniels earns him many enemies. So when one of them is found murdered, the police are on his doorstep within hours.

THE RED KNIGHT
Geoffrey Moxon

When he finds himself a pawn on the chessboard of international espionage with his family in constant danger, Guy Trent becomes embroiled in moves and countermoves which may mean life or death for Western scientists.

TIGER TIGER
Frank Ryan

A young man involved in drugs is found murdered. This is the first event which will draw Detective Inspector Sandy Woodings into a whirlpool of murder and deceit.

CAROLINE MINUSCULE
Andrew Taylor

Caroline Minuscule, a medieval script, is the first clue to the whereabouts of a cache of diamonds. The search becomes a deadly kind of fairy story in which several murders have an other-worldly quality.

LONG CHAIN OF DEATH
Sarah Wolf

During the Second World War four American teenagers from the same town join the Army together. Forty-two years later, the son of one of the soldiers realises that someone is systematically wiping out the families of the four men.

THE LISTERDALE MYSTERY
Agatha Christie

Twelve short stories ranging from the light-hearted to the macabre, diverse mysteries ingeniously and plausibly contrived and convincingly unravelled.

TO BE LOVED
Lynne Collins

Andrew married the woman he had always loved despite the knowledge that Sarah married him for reasons of her own. So much heartache could have been avoided if only he had known how vital it was to be loved.

ACCUSED NURSE
Jane Converse

Paula found herself accused of a crime which could cost her her job, her nurse's reputation, and even the man she loved, unless the truth came to light.

BUTTERFLY MONTANE
Dorothy Cork

Parma had come to New Guinea to marry Alec Rivers, but she found him completely disinterested and that overbearing Pierce Adams getting entirely the wrong idea about her.

HONOURABLE FRIENDS
Janet Daley

Priscilla Burford is happily married when she meets Junior Environment Minister Alistair Thurston. Inevitably, sexual obsession and political necessity collide.

WANDERING MINSTRELS
Mary Delorme

Stella Wade's career as a concert pianist might have been ruined by the rudeness of a famous conductor, so it seemed to her agent and benefactor. Even Sir Nicholas fails to see the possibilities when John Tallis falls deeply in love with Stella.

CHATEAU OF FLOWERS
Margaret Rome

Alain, Comte de Treville needed a wife to look after him, and Fleur went into marriage on a business basis only, hoping that eventually he would come to trust and care for her.

CRISS-CROSS
Alan Scholefield

As her ex-husband had succeeded in kidnapping their young daughter once, Jane was determined to take her safely back to England. But all too soon Jane is caught up in a new web of intrigue.

DEAD BY MORNING
Dorothy Simpson

Leo Martindale's body was discovered outside the gates of his ancestral home. Is it, as Inspector Thanet begins to suspect, murder?